THE RED TOQUE: LOVE AND LOSS IN THE TIME OF TITO

CYNTHIA HERBERT-BRUSCHI ADAMS

ISBNs:
Paperback: 978-1-64184-783-4
Ebook: 978-1-64184-784-1

Publisher: Strega Press

DEDICATION

To the Memory of
Rositha Por Adams

TABLE OF CONTENTS

ACKNOWLEDGEMENTS

It takes many people to assist in reconstructing history after most of the primary or first person participants are no longer available. Certainly acknowledging the authors that have recorded much of WWII itself and the strife of those times is essential. A list which was my bibliography for the historical portion of this novel is recorded on my website:

https://www.getbooksbycindy.com

And at this point I must thank **Michael Biggins**, Slavic, Baltic and East European Studies Librarian and Affiliate Professor, Slavic Languages and Literatures at the University of Washington, Seattle, for helping me to round out the scope of my research. He is also head of the Society for Slovene Studies to which my husband, Roger Andrew Adams, and I now belong. Their journal informed several points of the book.

In terms of family, **Roger Andrew Adams** was always my chief supporter, travel companion when we toured Germany, Austria and Slovenia in preparation for this book, and my first reader of each draft.

His first cousin, **Caroline Michaels** of London, UK, had wonderful memories not only from her mother but of much of the family due to opportunities her mother provided. Her accounts, photographs, and willingness to share ideas were a phenomenal help. Their cousin once removed, **Marija Andjelkovic Novakovic**, from Belgrade, knew many details having grown up knowing about her mother's missing father and having known Lovro's widow, her grandmother. She also was willing to talk and to share photographs and slip a few of her ideas into the mixture. And **Marko Por**, also a first cousin once removed, whose father, and grandfather (Janez) had told him the family stories, was also helpful. He and his daughter are the only direct descendants we found still living in Slovenia.

Our hosts at the Pletna Apartments and B & B in Bled were generous with their time and excited for us as we explored Bled in search of the original homestead and the family cemetery. Their mother, who was born just before the war started, knew answers to many of our questions and her grandson, Vid, would drive us anywhere. We have continued to correspond about this book and books as suggested readings for my preparation to write. **Antoija Music** (ne: Mandelc) the matriarch; **Mojca Music** as the catalyst for inspirations with **Robert Krasovec**, and their son, **Vid** who was knowledgeable and a great tour guide. Mojca could also proofread the little German I attempted to use. Their family is multilingual. "Danke."

My readers: Number one, as always, is **Ann Aulerich** who went through every chapter as it was written to provide acceptable punctuation and sage construction advice. She is generous with her time and support of the writing. **Caroline Michaels**, our cousin mentioned above, is also an excellent proofreader and understands the history and context. **Sharon Cormier**, a cousin in our US extended family, and herself an author, reviewed the entire manuscript and found several places where I had mixed something up or misused a word. I am indebted to her. **Jasminka Ilich**, a former colleague from the University of Connecticut, was born and educated in Yugoslavia. She read my earliest drafts to provide feedback on authenticity and she provided acceptable names to be used for characters in this region as I did not want all names to be taken from our actual family. And the final edit by a retired editor friend, **Sharyn Mathews**, who doesn't miss a thing, and provided me with the courage to finally, let the manuscript go. It takes a posse and I am truly fortunate!

I was also concerned about Marjana's (Vilma's) trip on the high seas during war times. It is a true story so I checked my understanding of it with **Lieutenant Commander John Lefebvre**, USN Retired, to be certain I did not misspeak of the ships probable operating instructions. I thank him for his help.

Priscilla and John Douglas provided some of the first books I would use to read about this time period and Slavic life; and neighbors **Eva and Yaakov Barshalom** discussed experiences that they and their families experienced within the war and in nearby Hungary.

Finally, my hat is off to a fellow writer of Slovenian historical fiction, **Margaret Walker**, whose book "His Most Italian City" was a shining example of the possibilities for our generation to write about this era. Her book is definitely worth a read.

INTRODUCTION

World War II brought many people together who would not otherwise have met. One cohort of this phenomenon is "The War Brides," who resulted from the mixture of soldiers, predominantly men, with women not of their own country. For my family, this is a matter of personal interest as my mother was an Italian woman who married an American GI from New Hampshire. Likewise, my husband is the result of an American soldier from Vermont marrying a Slovenian woman whom he met in London. World-wide this contributed to the post war "Baby-Boom" as did the simple return of the soldiers to their homes.

But the loss of six million Jews, the bombings all over the world, including Hawaii and Japan, and the countless other lives lost in the war, taint the thoughts of the romance by so meeting. And when one examines the details of this war, there was torture, pain and suffering inflicted as war crimes which remained largely hidden from the public eye. Even murders and other atrocities were dusted under a red carpet for nearly fifty years. A few were aware of the crimes and murders in 1945, just as the war had "ended;" but many secrets were held for fear of retribution. Hundreds of thousands met deaths so horrid they defy imagination yet are now documented. And even when described by first person reporters, it remains nearly impossible to believe that so much additional bloodshed occurred as brother sought revenge upon brother; the revenge for perceived wartime crimes would be acted out with a vendetta. Many could not let the war be over until they took retribution of the most horrific nature.

As the war began, those who had resources to inflict pain and death did so with the establishment of concentration camps, the raising of armies, and the dropping of bombs. Those that had no resources were said to use hammers and nails creatively. And the more personal nature the inflicting of pain involved, that is the killer was staring into the eyes of the victim, the more gruesome was the nature of the crimes; for, in many, a bloodlust arose which, once unleashed, overcame God and humanity within these beings.

Those whose blood was shed or whose families were executed would bear witness, and for generations remain enraged and internally corrupted by these traumas. But there were many families for whom deaths remain a mystery even unto this day. The father who made contact in May 1945 to say he was heading home, but was never heard from again. The farmer who traveled to the city for supplies, and returned home two weeks later without his horse or wagon only to report he had narrowly escaped alive and could not discuss more. There were locals who observed the beatings, and outright disposal of countrymen, and women, but who remained silent due to the sheer terror of those executioners. These are the stories, some recently told for the first time, which arise after generations of dust have settled; once citizens dare to speak.

We read that the United States entered the war late. It was late. To a great extent, the people of the United States wanted to protect their sons and daughters from the horrors of war; and, in part, due to cognitive dissonance, the actions in the concentration camps were too insane to believe. These acts defied credulity. It was easy to believe that the tales from camps were rumors, horrible rumors. And even so, documents were slipped out of the camps which validated these rumors.

In Europe, due to the events of the war, communication was severely limited, and stories of the torturous murders were available only via word of mouth. But in the United States there were more first-person accounts; people would escape or spy on an area and know for certain what evil was taking place even if they did not know its depth and breadth. Not until our Allies were approaching the end of hope, and Pearl Harbor was bombed, did we act. Thank God we did. Although the price was great, it was not so damning as ignoring the plight of the rest of the world.

This is a work of historical fiction. It is based upon actual occurrences, and several of the characters were members of the author's extended family. Several of the children and grandchildren of these individuals, as well as other Slovenian people, have contributed to this work.*

We will begin this novel in the month of November, 1912. This was the date of my mother-in-law's birth, and, is a representation of the lives of much of her family of six children. I have taken liberties with some details, but based these accounts on possible experiences from that time. The family who owns the pletna, and reside now in Bled, are not blood relatives but good friends whose lives give additional spark to "The Red Toque."

In the Epilogue, a detailed description is provided to clarify fact from fiction.

*Names provided in Epilogue

PART ONE

THE FAMILY

This is an historical novel. The Lovrenc Family (not actual names, but dates correspond roughly to the family being represented fictionally.)

Andrej (father)	b 1868
Justa (mother)	b 1881
Julijana (daughter)	b 1898
Mojca (daughter)	b 1900
Andrej II (son)	b 1904
Ivan (son)	b 1907
Rositha (daughter)	b 1912
Vilma (daughter)	b 1914

1

FIRST MEMORIES

Rositha woke up as she usually did, with the smell of porridge beckoning her to the kitchen below. Her mother always made a delicious mixture of buckwheat and warm cream. The bedroom she shared with baby Vilma was cozy this morning with light pouring in their window and reflecting back off the white stucco walls. The quilts on their beds, and the one hanging nearby, were cheerful using many vivid shades of red and turquoise offset by yellows and greens in embroidered scenes of lakes and flowers. They made a striking contrast with the stark white walls. The girls' clothing made little impact on the decor of the room, for it consisted of two wall hooks laden with dull green winter jackets and two soft wool hats which were dyed bright red. Their mother believed that the scarlet color helped to keep the children from losing them so easily. The remainder of their small wardrobe lay folded inside a three-drawer dresser near the side of Rosie's bed. She had under-clothing, two smocks, and a sweater within these drawers. Vilma still had only diapers and baby shirts. Both of Rositha's outfits had belonged to her big sisters Julijana and Mojca.

As part of a family with six children, Rositha and Vilma were fortunate to have their own bedroom even if it was so small that much of the room would not allow an adult to pass through it due to the height of the ceiling; their little room was tucked up under the eaves. Rositha's earliest memories were of being awakened by her crying baby sister, for there was no place which would permit her to be separated from the sounds of the hungry baby. But as Rositha grew, she could observe just how lucky her family was. On the outskirts of the town there were families who lived all together in one room, sharing a bed among them; and even poorer families who camped around fires they built in temporary locations. They would have to move frequently as they did not own the land nor pay rent to stay there; therefore, they must move before the actual owners would require the law to push them off the premises. These folks were called Gypsies and were looked down upon by much of the community. A little girl in her cozy bed would not wish to live this way even though she did learn to care about all people.

The other bedrooms were also small but clean and cheerful with the same white walls and colorful decorations. They reflected the needlework of the region's folk art with the bright colors of the countryside in which they lived. It has been said that there are no more beautiful places on earth than are found in Bled. The rich blue lakes reflect this hue with more color than an Aryan's eye and may be viewed from varying heights and depths: the green of the hills, and the azure of the water enhance the responses to these colors through the contrasts. And always the white tips of the mountains which surrounded them; some were actually snow while most were barren stone where no tree could grow.

The lower mountains had no white, just pine scented green. If one were to beat heavy cream until it thickened there would appear a series of thick, soft waves indicating it was now whipped cream. And so, this must have been how God made the mountains, as the soft green peaks of the trees were so thick and close together that they were as whipped cream peaks, softly flowing into each other.

Below these are flat areas where a true town emerged around the lake, but for many the ideal home was on the side of a hill with a view of the lake. Lake Bled was blue and crystal clear forming the center of their universe. In the middle of the lake was an island large enough to contain a small farm. Farming on such an island would be impractical. The farmer would have to ferry his animals and crops to market and transport feed and all supplies over to the island, so it appeared to have remained empty until about 1465 when Henry II donated the area to the church.

However, when excavating began on the island in preparation for construction of the church, there were a few surprises. Artifacts of campsites were unearthed, as well as the remains of more than one hundred skeletal bodies. The bones were then interred behind glass in the church, and some of the artifacts are on display in the nearby castle. Later, earthquakes required that the church be rebuilt in 1509 and again in 1747. The island holds many legends but was a particular favorite of Maria Theresa, Empress of Austria-Hungary, who ruled this area. Pilgrimages were frequently made to this church known by several names including The Assumption of Mary.

The small farm on which Rositha lived hovered above this church and the farm also had a view of the ancient castle on the cliffs which was 1,000 years old at the time of her birth. Their farm turned its sheep loose into the mountains for grazing on the sweet grasses and flowers during the short summer months. It was a respite for the children who would then not need to feed these animals for a while. Like the practical child she was to become, Rositha was learning that the value of the sheep is in their fleece, which would be shorn and then spun into yarn so that more coats and hats could be made. And perhaps once per year, generally at Easter, they would harvest an older ewe for a feast. Her fat would then be used for oil lamps, the making of tallow candles, and cooking grease.

Being told by her mother what the future was for all the sheep, helped Rositha to control an urge to feel maternal towards them. She saved her love and sweetness for her baby sister, and one of her older brothers, Ivan, who was not only handsome and sunny in his disposition, but willing to give her rides on his sled, and always made her laugh. Still, she loved Andrej Jr. too, as he cuddled the sheep. He was willing to shear their fleece, but he was never available when one of them was to be slaughtered. Apparently, he had given them names and cared too deeply for all animals.

In addition to the cheery bedrooms, their home was practical and efficient. Heat came up the middle of the house through a central chimney which also provided energy for cooking. It helped that their home was compact, as the glow of heat off the chimney stones had to provide enough warmth to keep them alive during the winters when wood ran low. Also, in winter the sheep slept in a small wooden pen right next to the doorway. If a night was thought to be too cold, the sheep would be herded into the kitchen area and blocked off from the rest of the house. This had the effect of keeping the sheep warm and the sheep helped to raise the temperature of the house, although perhaps not the air quality.

The staircases and woodwork were all from native trees and were roughly hewn by her father who had many skills. He was an excellent carpenter and well known in the area as a roofer. This trade helped to pay their bills. He constructed many shelves and wooden pegs. These were not intended for adornment but for practicality; coats and jackets would be hung to dry out on the mantle-like boards near the kitchen hearth, railings simply protected those climbing the stairs from a potential fall, and other boards made storage shelves and a place on which to prepare a meal or put out cheeses. Some of the boards high up on the kitchen walls, or running across the ceiling like beams, would alternately serve as either drying racks for clothing or curing spots for meat and cheese; and often, a combination of both. Still others held large nails and were used for securing the yarn once the fleece was cleaned.

These practical features had one aspect that might be considered frivolous by some cultures but were an absolute necessity to most families in the area. Over every doorway and the fireplace was a carved wooden crucifix. This necessitated the children to cross themselves frequently, especially while they were studying for their Holy Communion, and it gave their mother great comfort. It was all part of the reinforcement of the church as the cornerstone of their lives, which was helpful for what lay ahead.

The yard itself was dotted with several wooden racks standing at least six feet tall and of varying widths. These racks contained thirty or more rungs and were left as natural wood and weathered to a medium gray. Their use was for drying the hay when it was first harvested. It could then be stored in the barns much more safely. The grounds were also dotted with manure heaps. Their father tried to pile the excrement downwind of the house, which was an important consideration, but it also needed to remain where it could be most useful in fertilizing the soil for future grass and vegetable growth.

Rositha enjoyed the evening mealtime most when her dad might be home. All of the children gathered at the table, the girls helping her mother to serve her brothers. Early on, she recalled being admonished because she sat to eat before her oldest brother had a chance to receive his plate which usually consisted of venison, potatoes, and cabbage. She was told that the men worked hard all day planting or chopping wood or hauling rocks and building walls. Even if they were still boys, they needed to have the most food, and a girl should always wait, hold back from rushing to eat, and be sure to see what her father or brothers might require. In this way, her mother added, she would also learn to be a good wife and care for her husband properly.

Rositha didn't know that there might be any other way to look at the issue of who eats first and how much is fair. This is what they told her, and, in the beginning, it was not a problem for she wasn't hungry, just a thin child who was inclined to be respectful and did not demand things for herself. But she became a bit curious about what might be going on in other places as her parents sometimes spoke quietly of "more supplies being needed for the front; and how fortunate they were to live close to the land where one could fish, hunt, grow vegetables and have eggs when they needed them."

She wondered what was meant by this "front" and how it could affect them on their pretty side hill where everyone had cheese, flour, stuffed cabbages, and sauerkraut. And why her mother, who hardly had time to cuddle baby Vilma, would sometimes hold her brothers around their necks and say a little prayer of thanks that they were too young to go, followed by crossing herself. "Too young to go where?" she wondered.

Whatever was going on she did not much think about it as she had little jobs to do helping her mother, and occasionally found the time to let herself roll down the hill until she crashed into the fence which kept their garden from spilling into the lake. On the really good days, one of the older children would take her with them to have a quick swim before dinner. Those were wonderful summer days when no bath would be needed, and her hair would feel silky soft from lake water. It was light brown and would hang straight around the tops of her shoulders when it was freshly washed this way. Slipping into the lake also meant there was less water to haul and heat for the family to get cleaned that night. Their mother never wanted them to go to bed without washing first. She said it would ruin the bed linen which she was proud to own, as many families laid on coarse fabrics or sheep hides. And also, their mother believed that God wanted people to be clean in all they thought and did. Therefore, except on the coldest of nights, a bath was required.

Christmas was coming soon, and Rositha could only think of the red smock her sister Julijana had promised to alter so that she could wear it to church. Owning so little, a slight addition was appreciated and a cause for excitement. That, and she was having her fifth birthday very soon so that in another year she could possibly go to school with the bigger children. They had said so many things about Sister Maria Borislava that she wanted to see those "eyes in the back of her head" with her own eyes.

Be careful what you wish for little Rositha, you may be asked to grow up too fast.

2

PAPA ANDREJ

Andrej had found love and the opportunity for family, later in life, even by the standards of other Eastern Europeans. At the time he had married Justa, he wondered if he would be capable of fathering children, but soon after their little church wedding, she became pregnant with a daughter they named Julijana. It was a happy time, although his general demeanor and nature was to be quiet and a bit stern. Still, this baby made him laugh, and he could see why the women were always fussing over these little creatures.

He, however, had to pay attention to provide the food, and care for the land they needed to live a healthy life. His life had started out with little in material goods. All the people in his village were peasants, although he had owned his farmland. Very few others actually owned their land. Andrej and Justa were living a simple life off that land and building their own shelter. He soon became very capable in building so that others would pay for his help, especially when it was time to put on their roofs. But the locals were all mostly subsistence farmers; you planted what you needed to survive. Still, over time, they would have an understanding with some neighbors so that one might grow more grapes, and another more vegetables, and in this way, they could share, or trade, allowing each to produce what they did best, or what their particular land grew most easily.

Beyond their villages, there was government control influencing what could and could not be done. Austrian rule made it possible for many things to be organized, such as a community group which practiced putting out fires, and made it possible to deliver mail further than one's own village. This organization also brought with it an insistence upon knowing something called a census, allowing the government to command a duty, or tax, for every head over age six. Again, the census and taxes assisted both the Catholic Church, and the State of Austria-Hungary, in offering schooling for children.

Andrej was about thirty-five years old when attending school became a requirement. He was willing to send his children, as they came along, but he could already write and read a little himself. He managed to do what he must, and had a good command of numbers, which worked well enough for him. He kept his animals in order, and sold his services on the roofs, and fish for a fair price, and, of course, there was the pletna.

Pletna is the Slovenian word for gondola, and Maria Theresa had commissioned the building of several of these boats because they were a generous size for transporting groups of people across Lake Bled to her church, The Assumption of Maria. This became a sacred pilgrimage for many Catholics. The pletna was built so that it had a row of seats along each side and had a roof or canopy over the top allowing for pleasant transportation even when the weather was inclement. Maria Theresa had wanted these boats available whenever her pious followers, especially the clergy, might wish to pray in her church.

She was most entrepreneurial and commissioned several of the local farmers with good building skills to construct these boats and serve her pilgrims' needs. This had been initiated during the early part of her reign as Wife and Empress of the Holy Roman Empire in about 1740. Among the farmers she chose to do this building, and to captain her pletna, was a direct ascendant of Andrej, who then, by law, would pass the right to build and own pletna on to his sons, and to their sons (or daughters) in perpetuity. Thus, Andrej would count this role among his responsibilities.

Initially, he had resented paying taxes that disappeared over the miles to Vienna, but he had a more agreeable sense of things when he received his quarterly stipend from the State for maintaining his pletna; and, of course, he also accepted small gratuities from the worshipers who used them. During the Great War (later known as the First World War) there were also those who would pay well for special trips. He sometimes wondered if this island, which housed the beautiful church, was also a location for secret meetings, for no one could get on or off the island without being seen thus limiting the potential for spies. Perhaps they could silently row out and back at night if they had a boat, but they would have to come ashore and obtain housing or transportation from someone. Thus, no one on the island would be surprised by uninvited guests; those on the island could assume a certain protected intimacy like the eagle on its nest. Any intruders would be observed.

Some of the tipping provided to Andrej was due to Andrej's knowledge of the best places to fish on this small lake. Of course, growing up on the lake, and fishing every day, made it possible for his family to always know where the fish were, or how to bait them to come to a certain spot. They would leave small amounts of food leading to a favorite area, to which they would take the visitors. This would be done shortly before the guided tour was to take place, and extra baiting could occur as the visitors began to fish. Andre, Jr. and his father were not made wealthy by this, but they did "all right" they would say to their friends.

There were also many travelers who wished to visit the castle which was some distance from where their boats were docked. The climb to the castle was precipitous so that Andrej Jr. would meet his father's passengers when they arrived on land at the foot of the castle. They would then be driven in his wagon along a twisty switchback road to the back of the church which sits right under the castle. Many were advised not to look down the hill as the wagon meandered up the steep climb, for fear would surely cause them to panic. Once at the church, the painful climb into the castle was quite diminished.

⚬⚬⚬

Andrej and Justa had completed their family with the birth of their fifth and sixth children, Rositha, 1912, and Vilma, 1914, when Austria's Archduke, Franz Ferdinand, and his wife were assassinated in Sarajevo, the capital of Bosnia, in 1914, finally leading to the outbreak of The Great War. This quickly changed many things for the family as they lived in Austria-Hungary and were politically considered Austrians.

There was no electricity for the use of radios in Andrej's home, but his frequent contact with the outside area through the tourists seeking boats brought him much information. For as long as he had been conscious of the world, stories had arrived describing the fighting in neighboring areas. In fact, for fifty years prior to the outbreak of the Great War, there had been frequent conflicts in which the major powers were engaged. Also, the money spent on military prepared-ness, and the number of men conscripted to serve their countries as a military force, had risen year after year. Countries seemed to consider it their right to grow across their neighbor's borders and, following somewhat the mind-set of social Darwinism, the belief was one of survival of the fittest, not one of living in peace and harmony. That is, if a country could be conquered, then it was the conqueror's right to possess it; might makes right.

Too many ethnic groups had long-held animosities toward each other. These dislikes have been traced back to the earliest of days when different sects went from living in isolation, to then having frequent access to each other. What looked like an advantage for increased trade and support often resulted in increasing animosity and desta-bilizing the area. The great Nobel Literature-winning book, "The Bridge Over the Drina" by Ivo Andric told the history beginning in 1571, when this bridge was completed, and its impact on the areas it touched. If Turks built a bridge that enhanced transportation and communication, they also appeared to feel others should be grateful to them, and were obliged to follow their rules, especially around the use of the bridge, for example. But, the actual reaction of other groups, who appreciated the bridge in many ways, was to resent those who built it, for it changed their sense of themselves. They did not wish to show gratitude to the Turks, and could think of many reasons why they were better off without so much worldly contact.

One reason was safety: opening access to them geographically made many people feel unsafe, and the day would come when the bridge, for example, was used not only by warring factions, but for the enforce-ment of rules, regulations, and taxes by the dominant countries. Small peasant businesses which could get along with their neighbors when the countryside was limited in scope, and when all around you might be needed to support each other in an emergency, did not welcome too much trade, or the competition which would enter their town over that bridge. Soon the old customs and beliefs were crowded out and violence might occur. Further, a business which survived on a minimalist level; that is, they worked to sell only as much as they had to in order to eat and heat their homes, now had also to earn enough to cover taxes. The taxes helped, to some extent, to protect the business from factions that could not previously have entered the area, so the bridge was no longer all value-added, but a handicap.

Andrej and his family, living around the magnificent area of Lake Bled which he had always called home, were simple peasants with simple dreams only of taking care of their basic needs. They wished to have decent shelter, sufficient food, and an opportunity to grow and love each other. But the complexity of the struggle within the area surrounding them, and throughout this Eastern European/Balkan part of the world and beyond, would threaten them all.

The Serbs believed the Croatians could never be right, and the Croatians believed that the Serbs were always wrong according to some authorities. Nothing could resolve such hard-held beliefs. This thinking would almost be humorous if so many lives were not to be lost. Yet, the part of the world that became known as Yugoslavia ten years after World War I, following the postwar name of "Kingdom of Serbs, Croats and Slovenes" (1918-1929) was fraught with these conflicts.

Religion, as well as national origin, played an enormous role in fostering and perpetuating the animosities of the region. Hatred of the Turks translated into an intense dislike of Muslims in general. The Catholics believed that they were entitled to hold power over all groups as they represented God. The priests not only used their power to provide better schools to those who were the TRUE Catholics, and not some bastardized version called Orthodox, but they became so involved in governing and control that they ordered the slayings of some of those who opposed their thinking.

Andrej would not know all of this, for much, especially regarding the roles of the priests during the war; and the need for secrecy for the crimes at the end of the war, would remain hidden until later years. When Andrej floated out on beautiful Lake Bled with people headed on their pilgrimages, they would occasionally speak too freely of the sins they had seen committed, and of their fears for the future of the entire region. Andrej had much to think about for a man who worked all day with his hands.

And finally, he held one secret dear. Some of his ancestors, not so far back, had held special roles as established by Napoleon Bonaparte. Napoleon conquered this area in 1797 and maintained control until his banishment at Waterloo in 1814. He did many good things for the area during that short time including treating people equally under the law, making taxes uniform and separating the Church from the State in terms of governance. He also gave the Slovenes an important gift: not only did he promote education, but he allowed Slovene to be used as an acceptable language in school. Prior to this only French, Italian and German had been permitted as acceptable languages. This was a magnificent gift to the Slovenian people. Specific families had been thanked and honored by Napoleon, although they were not in positions to continue to hold themselves above their fellow Slovenes as a coat of arms was only of value while Napoleon governed. Still, Andrej had been told by his father, and passed this on to his children, that they should hold their heads high, for there was something noble about them. The children certainly enjoyed this intrigue.

3

MAMA JUSTA

Justa had been born on a farm not far from Bled. She was the third of eight children, the first girl, and naturally hers was a Catholic family, which helps to explain the number of children even though the family could barely feed them all. But her parents had been clever in their attempts to manage this brood. They believed that the best way for children to grow up to be sensible was to keep them busy. Justa's oldest two brothers worked continuously on clearing more fields by rolling rocks to the edge of an area, and then building stone walls to surround and protect that area. They soon trained the younger two brothers, and all four of them would hunt deer and rabbits early in the day as well as at dusk and build walls in the middle of the day.

Her sisters spun yarn from the sheep. Her mother and grandmother then put the yarn to use for heavy sweaters and coats that were a necessity in this typically cold mountainous area. And as early as Justa could remember, she had been working with bees. Her mother kept a beautiful flower garden which attracted and fed the bees enough for a few jars of honey each year. The bees loved

17

the sweetest smelling flowers and would descend by the hundreds upon the right groups of blooms. As the season changed, the bees would adapt; starting with Edelweiss and finishing the late summer with Tamarix plants which always provided so much nectar they were considered a miracle when nothing else was blooming. It was Justa's job to be sure the beehive was safe and to note when her Papa should harvest the golden liquid that then made room for more honey to be produced. He did this by removing the top basket so that the hive wasn't destroyed, and production could continue. Between the flowers and the honey, Justa could not think of a more pleasant job.

They all worked hard, and by doing so as a group, they were then able to share enough variety of food and commodities to live, if not well, at least to feel sated most days. Life went on nicely in this manner with struggles that seemed normal in the sense that they could be overcome in a few days rather than signaling a devastating situation. One such minor catastrophe occurred when Justa went out to check on the hive, and saw a bear stalking it as it slowly came over the hill moving towards the basket. The bear appeared fat, and its body rippled, as it climbed. Justa's instinct to scream, shout, hurl rocks, and to charge at the bear actually worked. But she was reprimanded as this behavior went against her parents' admonitions to avoid bears. Still, the honey that winter tasted all the sweeter knowing they had nearly lost a precious hive.

More serious was the occasional loss of a lamb to a predator. All of the family attempted to check on the sheep as often as they could, but when everyone is responsible, sometimes no one is responsible enough, and a quick moving predator, such as a wolf, would snatch a baby lamb and run. The result was almost as though the lamb had disappeared by magic, so suddenly and completely was it missing; only the plaintive bleating of the ewe, which was loud, mournful, and guttural, would confirm that a loss had occurred.

Still, if these losses were not too frequent, and with the addition of fish and game, the family did manage. The first real struggles began as the oldest boys wished to leave the farm to make their own way in the world. The loss, by now, of two grown men left a tremendous gap in production even subtracting the food that they would have eaten. But the younger two sons stepped up their efforts. Things would have gone more easily if their father had not started drinking plum brandy to compensate for the aches and pains of old age. By now, he was a very old man and took the brandy like lifesaving medication. While the brandy was cheap, there were days when their father did little else but drink.

This behavior hastened the inevitable decline of the man himself and left the remaining children with an anxious desire to find their own way out of the home. Soon the household was down to three children; one son, and two daughters, one of whom was Justa. And, in only a few more years, the burden of helping the parents seemed to fall exclusively on Justa, as all the others moved out for occupations at a distance, or to make families of their own. Being the oldest daughter, Justa felt she had little choice but to care for her parents.

She bore her duties without complaint, but her jaw was set hard in her face as though it would never move to laugh again. For her there was only work, worry and church. She clung to the Catholic services like a cocoon does to a tree. If it were not for the sweet smell of incense and the promises of the priests, she might not have been able to bear the dismal life of caregiver and farmhand which was now her lot. It seemed she must always be cleaning up after a parent or an animal with no time left for herself.

Then one night her father did not return home from the small tavern where he sat each evening drinking with his friends. It wasn't until morning light that a man delivering milk to a neighbor found her father's lifeless body partially covered in snow. It appeared he had tried to walk home and lost his way. They said he died with a smile on his face. Perhaps plum brandy left him happy; Justa hoped this was so for he had been a good father most of her life.

Now they were just two people, and she could not bear to leave her mother alone. Yet, one of the men who had been a drinking friend of her dad's, began to call on her. He said he was coming by just to see if he could be of help, if she needed anything fixed to which he might attend. This started to please her, and soon she was smiling. She allowed him to do a few things, and she would prepare a meal for him, but never offered brandy. They continued like this, as just friends, for over a year.

Finally, one evening, he told her more about himself, and that he wondered if she might not like to try to start a family with him. He said he owned land with a small wooden house on it and was soon intending to add a barn. It looked right out onto the lake, and to the castle on one side, he added, and would be a pleasant place for children if God granted them any.

Justa was pleased, having long been fearful that marriage and family would pass her by. This sounded like an opportunity to have a normal life. But she could not leave her mother, and told him so, although she thanked him kindly for thinking of her in this way. It surprised her that he was not interested in hearing "no" for an answer. He continued to explain how easy it would be to add space onto the house and that her mother was welcome to live with them. He said he wanted a house bursting with family, although at the time he said it, he might have been trying to convince himself as much as Justa.

When she said, "Yes, Andrej, I will marry you, and see what comes of it," he was as pleased as he would have been if she had declared her enduring love. He had never known, nor expected romance, but he appreciated hard work and a practical attitude, both of which he saw in Justa. He said they should speak to her mother, and then contact the priest. He added that at his age he had no time to waste if they wanted babies, and she declared her anxiousness to be a mother. And so, in the late 1890s, they became man and wife in a modest Catholic church not far from the small center of Bled.

The wedding was simple. Justa wore her best house dress with a lace apron tied about it and a lace cap on her head. She stole a few posies from the bees to carry into the ceremony, and a few friends, her mother and one sister attended the ceremony which was mostly a Catholic Mass. Then they were officially married.

Justa heard that wars were going on in other places not far from where they made their home. This information came from a few soldiers who would come by looking for a night's shelter, and a meal, or the people who took boat trips with her husband. They always found a way to help the desperate travelers to find food and a spot to sleep in with the sheep. Justa believed that God would protect her family from these strangers, and from war.

"After all," she reasoned, "We are but simple farmers who have nothing for which others would want to fight."

When the babies came, she endeavored to raise them with a firm hand, and a Catholic faith that would help protect them. She also followed the pattern established by her parents which immersed the children in hard work just as soon as they could manage it. With all this in mind she felt safe, and if not happy, at least at peace.

4

JULIJANA AND MOJCA

As the eldest of six children, Julijana felt that she had been born working. She was barely old enough to sit up herself when baby Mojca came along and was propped into her lap so that she could give her a bottle, thus permitting their mother the freedom to perform more complex tasks. While mother was making a stew, or running out to pump water, Julijana had to be certain that the baby was entertained so that there would be no crying. Their mother was wise enough to leave them against the wall in the main room so that they were not in danger of falling, but lately Julijana wanted to leave her sister and toddle over to wherever she could find her mother. A few attempts at this led to Mojca screaming and Julijana being corrected. Her mother was never angry with her, but she was firm; after all, there was work to be done.

By 1914, when her last sibling, Vilma, was born, fifteen-year-old Julijana was doing everything for the other children except lactating. Her hands were always red and coarse from doing so much laundry, her social life was limited to friends who didn't mind if they played with babies while visiting Julijana, and she was always tired as she had to help with the baking and sewing after the youngest ones were put to bed. The biggest impact all this responsibility may have placed on her life was that she quit school as soon as she completed the lower grades. She was twelve years old when she walked away from their school for the last time.

The nuns had protested, even coming by the house to speak with her parents; an almost unheard of gesture, but her mother could only agree that Julijana was needed at home. Mojca, on the other hand, had never been as patient with her siblings as was her big sister, and she was a brilliant student, so the holy sisters accepted that they could keep the other children in school, but had to release the eldest.

Once school was out of the equation of her life, Julijana filled her head with escape fantasies. She dreamed of what life must be like in Vienna from which she had learned of beautiful music and glamorous opera halls. Ladies wore long silken gowns to go out with gentlemen in black suits, and they dined in places adorned with spectacular crystal chandeliers. And the sky all around the city was filled with the peaks of buildings not mountain tops. How she yearned to see what an actual city was like, and one so historical and, to her thinking magical, as Vienna. Perhaps she would even glimpse an Empress if she managed to travel there.

Then The Great War interceded, and she was stuck in place until it was over, and the danger passed. She had asked her father how she might make some money to begin to save for her future. He had told her that her sweet rolls might sell well to the pilgrims who sought transportation in his pletna. They came, although not so frequently, even though the war was on, and he could provide the buns in his boat with a note indicating their cost. To her amazement, each week he brought her a few coins and asked for more rolls. Although he did not know he was aiding and abetting her escape, he was proud of her.

What made her confections so popular was not simply based on the hunger of the pilgrims, but her use of the honey she and her mother produced on their farm. Her mother had passed this craft on to all her girls, and Julijana was simply the first to put it to use outside of the few jars they would always sell at the market.

Those coins added up to enough, she supposed, for a one-way train ticket to Vienna. But the war was raging, and the trains were either being used by the military, or by soldiers who had pulled up the tracks to stop supplies from being transported. The ties were then burned to keep someone warm in their makeshift camps, or at a poor farm not far away.

And at home it was nearly Christmas. Julijana had to repair a pretty dress for Rositha, make one new dress for Mojca, who was now her size so secondhand clothing was not available, make a cloth doll for little Vilma, and figure out what to do for Andrej the second and for Ivan. Ivan was crazy about trains. He seemed to miss the whistle of the train which used to bring visitors to the lake for it too was disabled by the war. But their father had told them of a man who sat near the boats working with wood all day. Her plan was to see if he would make a little train for Ivan which she could then paint and surprise him with on Christmas day.

Andrej, her brother, liked to think of himself as a guardian of the family. They had dogs that kept watch over the sheep, but Andrej wanted to keep watch over the dogs, and all people who might trespass on their farm. He thought the war might bring rough people from a rough country into their area. He believed it to be his duty to see that his sisters, and younger brother, were not bothered by these men whom he had really not seen, but had a sense of in his mind.

In his imagination he pictured a dull colored uniform with many rips and tatters hanging around the legs of a thin young man. This soldier was always angry and hungry so he would take what he wanted, robbing a family of a whole pie by stealing it off of a window ledge where it might have been set to cool, or walking into a barn and dipping his hand into a pail of honey or taking raw eggs out from under the chickens. Andrej was too young to understand what more horrible things these soldiers might actually do. He knew virtually nothing about rape and the burning of a farm simply to deprive the enemy of its bounty. Murder was only something that occurred when the soldiers were in face-to-face combat; he understood nothing of the sneaky, desperate, stabbing of another in the back to acquire their possessions, and to walk away with valuables which were not his own.

For this reason, Julijana asked the man who whittled to carve her both a train and a gun. She thought she could make each brother happy with these gifts. But much to her disappointment, the wood-carver wanted money instead of rolls, or even a jar of honey. And the cost for these two items was exactly what she had saved up for her train fare. Since the trains were stopped, and the dangers of travel far too great for a young woman alone, Julijana was able to make the decision to buy the gun and train for her brothers as their holiday gifts. As she handed the coins over to the man on a December evening when a cool breeze was flowing over Lake Bled, and there was snow in the air, the shiver she felt went deeper than her skin, and left a true chill, but she would not reconsider her determined resolution to make this a wonderful Christmas for their whole family.

Mojca loved the pletna; she pleaded with her father each time he was headed for his docks that she should join him and would be of great help to him, and couldn't she please go along? This began before either of her brothers was of an age to be helpful, so he saw no harm in allowing a girl to assist in pushing the boats out and started to teach her to row. Although she was slender, she was growing fast, and with just a little direction she seemed to understand movement and safety in the water. These were essential for anyone giving rides to the pilgrims. She was also a pretty girl, all of his daughters would be, with light hair and skin tanned from exposure on the water. It was easy for her to charm the travelers. She quickly learned to tell them the history of the Lady of the Lake, and of Maria Theresa's love of this church and the Slovenian people.

According to legend, in about 1100, the Lord of the area was murdered by thieves and disposed of in Lake Bled not far from the island. When word of this was sent to his castle hanging above the lake, his wife, the Lady of the Lake, mourned so intensely that she sold all the gold she had, and any that would be donated by those who also loved the Lord, to make a bell for the church on the island to ring in his honor.

As the bell was being brought to the island, a sudden storm arose that sank the little ship, its cargo, and killed the captain. Divers attempted to find the bell, but it was too heavy and had sunk to the bottom of the lake. Overwhelmed with even more grief, the Lady left the Castle and moved to a monastery in Rome where she lived out her life in prayer.

Upon her passing, the Pope of the time learned of her story and commissioned a bell for the tower with which he traveled to be certain it was hung at The Assumption of Maria Church on the island. It still hangs there and is for ringing by those who believe in God, for it gives them good luck. As for the original bell, the legend states that on certain nights, if you are walking near the lake, you may hear its sound as a low, almost hollow tone that vibrates deep from within the water.

Nearly every person on the trips who heard Mojca tell this story would be certain to ring the bell left by the Pope, and to hope they might hear more if they were staying close-by that night. She was also a wonderful student, so her father saw to it that she did not leave school to work at his side, but he scheduled as many trips as possible when he knew she could accompany him. Mojca was not only beautiful and clever, but the rowing she began at such an early age led to her becoming athletic and strong which would be of value to her on many occasions.

Sometimes, while wars are taking place, a clever woman may pass in the night and achieve heroic feats simply because no one will imagine that she could accomplish them. And perhaps the ringing of the bell saved her more than once.

5

CHRISTMAS 1917 IN THE LITTLE HOUSE IN BLED

The War continued all around them and could be felt each day. Some days it was a distant cloud rising over the mountains as though a fire of great intensity was burning; some days it was a poor starving soldier appearing at the door begging for food and drink; sometimes it was even a man on horseback from one of the regiments checking to be certain no able-bodied male was hiding on the farm. This visitor would cause fear if he was recruiting more soldiers rather than checking for deserters. They did not know how they would manage without their father if he should be commandeered to fight. The oldest son was barely twelve and was followed by his ten-year-old brother; not enough muscle to run the farm, manage the boats, and build roofs even if the women could tend the sheep, care for the bees and vegetables, in addition to managing childcare and the household. The "simplicity" of the old days must be viewed with a sense of what it would really be like to perform so many jobs to earn a living to support a family of eight, and how difficult those chores would be without running water, electricity or modern farm equipment.

The size of this family, the youth of the children, and the advancing age of their dad spared them the loss of their father to fighting in The Great War. But, a future war may always be anticipated in this region, one which would command a sacrifice from all. Still, on this occasion of Christmas 1917 Andrej and Justa were grateful that they could manage the sacrifices asked of them thus far, and they were joyful that they had a houseful of happy, loving children as the centerpiece of their holiday. The church was important to them all in varying degrees, but Justa, especially, loved the holiday rituals and had saved a little extra for her offering this time of year.

Being so close to Germany, where many Christmas traditions had originated, and surrounded by trees, it had also become a custom in Slovenia to decorate a "Christmas tree." But the relative smallness of their house when all were home, made it too crowded to have a traditional large tree in the center of a room decorated with many items. The heating system also dictated that the family must be careful, or a decoration could easily become a firebomb. So, the family chose a small tree, possibly even a portion of a larger tree, to place in a dirt filled bucket which they would endeavor to keep moist. It was situated on a wooden table nearly in the center of the great room and at considerable distance from the wood stove. It could be enjoyed from every angle on the ground floor without drying out too quickly. One of the girls was always sticking her fingers into the pot to ascertain if there was a need for watering as this was a serious chore to maintain until Christmas. After that, the tree would be placed outside and suet would be tied to it to entertain the birds, although sometimes neighbors would request the trees to feed their goats or donkeys.

The ground in Bled was already covered in snow. It was a cold region with the temperatures declining, back in those days, nearly as soon as it became September. But even though snow was fairly plentiful, the lake was not so frozen over that it could be trusted to take much weight. Thus the pletna were still used for a few fall months to ensure the safety of a crossing to the church. That meant that Mojca and her father used their horse and plow to scrape paths around the lake leading to their dock, but did not use the heavy horse and plow on the lake itself.

Meanwhile, as it grew nearer to Christmas, the younger children were excited because it was one of those rare times when they might anticipate receiving treats. Certainly, the little girls observed their oldest sister sewing things that might be for them, and their mother was concocting something special with the honey which could turn out to be candies rather than throat medicine. This scrutiny of what others might be preparing led the littler children to make attempts at preparing gifts themselves. Rositha and Vilma took a basket from the shed, often used to collect the chicken eggs, and brought it to the edge of the forest quite near their farm where many pinecones lay fallen and ignored. They harvested the healthier looking of these cones to present to their mother and Julijana to aid in starting fires as they had observed them both using. Rositha was old enough to distinguish between the older, rather beat up appearing cones, which might have been on the ground for quite some time judging by the mushiness of some of the scales on the cones, and the healthier ones. Also, these older cones would be challenging to dry out, and not attractive when presented in a basket.

The biggest difficulty for these little girls in harvesting pinecones was in retrieving them before the snow significantly buried them, or made walking close to the woods too challenging for the children. But once they saw their mother and sister busily at work, they managed to acquire what was needed. Then Rositha and Vilma, these two little roommates, began to whisper about St. Nicholas and what they might actually find under their tree even though they knew not to expect too much.

Potica bread was a guaranteed treat. On Christmas day the meal would be enhanced by this special bread which their mother baked each year. It was yeast bread that one would knead after it rose at least once, and then rolled or stretched it over the table top where the tree would eventually go. While it was pulled as far as it would go, the top was scattered with breadcrumbs, ground walnuts and butter mixed with honey. It was then rolled up and baked all as an important ritual of the holiday. It tasted fairly bread-like but was a treat. When St. Nicholas did arrive, the gifts were kept simple by necessity: everyone received apples, walnuts, and if lucky, an orange. The few gifts a parent or a sister might add to the occasion were a special touch but not anticipated or expected.

Before St. Nicholas would visit the family, all went to the little village church for midnight Mass. After the religious portion of the service, St. Nicholas would march in from the front of the church accompanied by an angel, usually one of the young girls from the parish. Then, from the back of the church, a man would appear who all knew to be the devil. He would be wearing heavy chains and making rattling sounds. He would pretend to chase after those who might have been bad during the year that was ending, then it would all end in laughter, and the families would go home to enjoy their own celebrations and see what might have been left for them.

On this Christmas Andrej Junior accepted the gift of the carved gun as a trophy. He knew it wasn't real, but it symbolized to him the respect he felt for the police and for doing things right. He loved the idea of order and the authority to keep things in order. He informed his siblings that they had better behave in the future with him around, and all laughed, but Andrej was smiling on the inside too for he felt more important and knew that he would be.

Certainly, each and every one of them was happy that year. They had enough to eat even if it were not luxurious, they were warm and had laughter, and, more than anything else, they had each other. The gifts given and received reflected the importance of their family more deeply than did the little treasures themselves. There was a happiness about which the older family members tried not to feel guilty. Not guilty because a family had the right to enjoy this love and they had sacrificed for each other; but guilty because all around them people were at war: and loss and sacrifice was so normal it could even be anticipated.

And, in an uncharacteristically fun-loving mood, Andrej Sr. presented the girls with a scrawny little puppy of which one of his roofing customers had been desperate to be rid. There was nothing wrong with the puppy; it was simply that they could not fathom another mouth to feed. When this matter was gently raised by Justa, Andrej stated that such a small animal could subsist on any scraps the children might leave on their plates. The girls squealed in unison "Oh, yes, papa yes, we can find enough food for him!"

And the matter seemed settled. They named him Tacek (Little Paw), and Andrej, Jr. took him outside to begin potty training as it was too cold, he said, for the girls to do it. Of course, they all thought that this was Andrej's way of seeking a chance to also play with the dear puppy. This dog was different than the ones that helped with the sheep for he was intended to live inside and to play with them to earn his keep.

6

THE GREAT WAR ENDS AND BRINGS CHANGE

By 1918, the Great War, thought to be so bloody and fierce that it would be "the war to end all wars" was over. Austria-Hungary, along with the Habsburg Monarchy, had collapsed, and much of Europe would be rearranged as one might redistrict a country: the countries, of course remained in the same locations, but their names and allegiances changed along with the countries' various leadership.

Slovenia was now part of the Kingdom of Serbs, Croats and Slovenes with Peter I of Serbia serving as the leader thus explaining the name "Kingdom of." Croatia and Slovenia seemed to favor a federal system of government and were mostly Roman Catholics; whereas Serbia was a supporter of a centrist government and fiercely demanded equal rights for their Orthodox religion. Perhaps, these differences could have been mitigated by a balanced governing system, but Peter I's leadership did not create a balance. One could feel the resistance mounting immediately when this leadership was announced: the idea of anything being equal was automatically suspect.

By definition, the centrists were well led by a king, for they believed power and government should be handled somewhere apart from the masses. The citizens went about their own business trusting a central government to make the proper decisions for them. However, the believers in a federalist system wanted an active role in how they were governed. They wished to be informed and to participate in the duties needed for their countries to function. These very disparate views may have been doomed to failure, especially when coupled with long-held negative views of the Serbs against the Croats and vice versa. This Kingdom of Serbs, Croats and Slovenes lasted from 1918 to 1929. The name Yugoslavia appeared after the term Kingdom beginning in 1929, and then the country would be known simply as Yugoslavia in 1945 under the leadership of Communist Josip Broz Tito.

Rositha was growing up fast, listening to the conversations of her father and older siblings, taking in some of the values seen in her Catholic school which favored Roman Catholics against the Orthodox, and absorbing, to some extent, the difficulties the war had brought with it. Certainly, the people of Serbia, Croatia, and Slovenia had wished to be independent of Austria-Hungary, but they suffered many sacrifices as this war continued. They were still required to pay taxes to the country from which they were trying to make a break; and they had to feed those who were fighting for independence, as well as being forced to assist any warriors who were near them.

Basically, the only way they were able to manage was that more of the children worked harder, and all of the family helped to raise more food while consuming less of it. If an Austrian "Tax collector" showed up at the farm, then there had better be wool, meat, honey, and cloth goods to compensate for the lack of cash. Rositha remembered evenings after school when her mother would send her out to the garden to find enough food with which to stretch dinner. They might have a little mutton and onion stewing in water, but it was necessary for Rositha to find perhaps a few carrots, and a potato to be included in the pot. One night she found a few string beans that were still growing under their leaves and delighted her mother by providing enough beans to break into the broth so that they could all have a taste. "Six people, twelve beans, it was a miracle!" she thought.

And so the lessons of war were learned the hard way. Through loss, deprivation, and fear that the next day, or the next week, might be worse, Rositha learned that life was serious and not magical as a young girl might wish to think of the world. Sometimes, at night when she was in bed with Vilma just a few feet away, they would tell each other stories of the dinner they would plan when things changed. There would be roast lamb and roast venison, steamed cabbage that was tender and sweet, a mountain of mashed potatoes, fresh carrots of a bright orange hue, and their sister's rolls dripping with honey and butter. Then they would sigh and say "Ah!" both thinking of someday.

Of course, a few miracles did happen that were bigger than the string beans. Their brothers Andrej and Ivan went into the forest one Saturday to hunt. It was after a week when the family had suffered through a very lean time by living only on omelets and beets. If things had become any scarcer, they feared their father would strangle a chicken, thus leaving them with even fewer eggs for the future!

But the boys were lucky. They had walked away from the house, and hopefully away from the scent of humans, but not so far in that the oak trees would disappear. Then they found an old log fronted in part by downed branches with some leaves remaining on them. By sitting on the log they managed to conceal themselves behind this brush and essentially had created a blind. They waited patiently, never speaking, only facing forward, alert to the sounds of birds and squirrels which chattered and cavorted all around them: the boys were busy cocking their heads to indicate to each other that something was making a noise, but also grimacing so that the other would know it was not likely to be their prey. They were hungry, so traveling further did not hold much enchantment. They waited.

And it would pay off. They had never before hunted deer without their father, but he was too busy to join them this day. He had reminded them of safety. Then they heard a crackling of leaves and a huffing, almost a barking sound, which signaled the entrance of a large buck to their area. It snorted again and scraped at acorns on the ground, then stopped and raised its head seeming to sniff at the breeze. The boys made not a sound but waited with their hearts beating very fast within their young chests, until the buck stepped directly in front of them into the clearing. It was red and held its eight-point antlers high.

Their guns sounded simultaneously; one bullet went into the buck's heart right behind its shoulder, the other only trimmed a little hair off from under its chest. Initially the boys were stunned as it dropped quickly with barely a step. Then both boys would claim to have delivered the critical wound, but no one would ever know that Andrej had intentionally missed. He knew the family needed meat badly, but he did not feel that he could take this sweet animal's life. At that moment he threw himself into acting, the family heard a great whooping sound from the edge of the forest as the boys came over the hill, both pulling for all they were worth to bring home that dead deer on a litter made of pine boughs.

The older girls ran toward the carcass while Rositha was sent to get her father. They thought as a team to get this great body out of the possible sight of the neighbors, or any passersby, and into the barnyard to be dressed, separated, hung, if necessary, for some parts, and hidden and stored from harm and view. The liver was quickly removed, and Vilma nearly gagged as she rushed the steaming organ into the kitchen and deposited it into a stew pot. As wretched as it looked to the young girl, she did understand that soon it would be cooked and delicious for the evening meal. Other organs, heart and kidneys, were similarly stewed with the neck and an onion to serve as the base for subsequent meals. This stock too, would be the hearty beginning of a vegetable soup capable of sustaining them beyond the weak vegetable broth that had to pass for a meal on many days.

The boys were bloody and tired, but about as happy as a couple of children could be. Not only had they shot the prize and delivered a substantial contribution to the family, but they would likely get warm boots from this hide. It was one moment and several days of good eating that would stay in their minds throughout the leaner days ahead. Mother already had plans for different parts to be salted and hidden away. The one thing they would not do was to mount the antlers even though this rack was impressive. Their fear was that someone might figure out how recently this kill had taken place and start demanding a portion of the meat. The family, to a one, could not tolerate the loss of this prize, which seemed a gift from God that they would not even mention to the priest.

Their sheepdog got bones for supper containing real meat, leftover liver was pulverized with a wooden spoon and spread on bread for lunches, and some of the broth was placed in a dark part of the cellar to help to preserve it for as long as possible. Liver toast and honey seemed a great luxury at this time.

PART TWO

A TIME BETWEEN WARS

7

JULIJANA REACHES FOR HER DREAMS

Hunger and ever-deepening poverty were what the war had brought to their area, which was now called The Kingdom of Serbs, Croats and Slovenes under Peter I, a Serbian. Yet the citizens were accustomed to the old ways. Although they may have desired freedom from Austria-Hungary, the price of such a change in governance was internal fighting over both the practice of managing themselves and the religions to be honored. There was more distrust and prejudice. In the pre-Great War days, the Habsburg Monarchy seemed overbearing but the citizens knew what to expect. Now that they were diminished in size, governed by a Serbian monarch, and still had no voice in their own affairs, many Croatians and Slovenians felt victimized while the Serbs felt victorious. The lack of equity, with the farmers' goods going to "feed the Monarch," left brother angry with brother.

There was enough internal turmoil during these times that it began to breakup families. Not only was there not enough food at home to feed many mouths, but there was also a lack of hope. Young people could not see a future in their homeland. What kind of life would it be to end up like their parents, and sweat all day in the fields, to then eat a meal so watered down and lacking in nutrition that you felt as though your throat was cut because your stomach remained so empty?

And what of romance, or the hope for one's own family; no one was courting as there were too many chores, and too little time to bathe and dress to be charming. Julijana was eighteen as the war ended yet she remained at home to help. She carried on her domestic duties in order to support her mother and siblings with all their burdens. But as she turned nineteen, she began to see her prospects dimming as though she were already a spinster of thirty with her womb drying up and her hair falling out, for this is how she had observed her mother to age even with a husband and children. While always respectful of the elderly, when she saw a wrinkled older woman with few teeth, and wild white hair, she imagined that a mirror was staring her in the face. She was feeling desperate about being trapped at home.

Even though their country was no longer tied to Austria, Vienna still existed right over the mountaintops. Since the Great War had ended, there was a train running much of the time that could take her out of this poverty and hopelessness and into a big city. Vienna had been badly injured by the war, but many important structures still stood. There were palaces and opera houses and merchants with glimmering products. There were artists and dancers and fine restaurants rebuilding. Everything she yearned to see lay just a mountaintop away and travel to these places would give her a freedom which she had never known.

Julijana was frightened, but not so scared that it destroyed her hope. She had never been far from home, or even away overnight without family members, but she yearned to see night lights and wear a ball gown once before she became a prune, she told herself. And so she added a job working for the church, doing cleaning for the priests, in order to accrue a few coins. The church was the only place where money could be found, as the peasants dropped their meager coins into the collection boxes even when they were unable to buy bread.

And Julijana had another advantage. In addition to being clever and strong enough to follow her dreams, she was very beautiful. All of the Lovrenc girls were considered handsome; with high cheek-bones and large warm eyes. Some had more prominent noses than others, but it gave them an aristocratic look along with their generally straight posture and strong bodies from the rugged farm life. She was considered statuesque. Many of the customers to the pletna had inquired about her even when she was a little child, but her father dismissed them all. There would be no talk of a betrothal for his little girl, and so she had remained a good Catholic child helping her family at home, but secretly yearning for a life with some adventure.

When she began working with the priests, she was amazed to see them lounging in the large brick home without wearing their sacred garments. She could scarcely believe that they were simply men as were her brothers, and she often blushed when they would walk by her barely covered as they headed outside to a bathing area. Well, she told herself, I am simply a piece of furniture to them, just a servant to do what must be done and to stay out of their way. And she operated with this assumption for many weeks.

But one Saturday in September, when the church was preparing for a huge festival, she was asked to work all day and to spend the night, for right after Mass the next day there must be booths ready to receive the parishioners' goods for the festivities, and games for the children. There would also be a pageant requiring a temporary walkway to be adorned with flowers and boughs of greens from the forest. Although there were many volunteers who helped in the planning of the event, and who carried the adornments into the church's courtyard in preparation, the holy Fathers, for there were two at this church, wanted Julijana to be sure everything went smoothly, and if there was anything requested by the volunteers, that she would make it available to them.

Since it was an overnight at the church, Justa and Andrej Sr., did not hesitate to grant their daughter permission to spend the night. Justa simply made certain her daughter carried a well mended nightdress with her so that no one need to think of her as shabbily clad. Julijana could not imagine that anyone but the live-in housekeeper, would even possibly see her, but she allowed her mother to help her to pack in this way. It was also only fifteen minutes to walk to the church from their farm so that Julijana could not imagine that she would require much.

After the evening meal within the priests' home, which Julijana assisted in serving as she did not know what to do with herself, the priests then went to pray. She began pulling boxes of supplies and contributed decorative materials out of cupboards, back closets, and hallways; some of the material was also stored in an alcove at an administrative building, and under tarps which had earlier been left in the courtyard. Time passed, and the sky was darkening. The younger priest came out with a workman, and they began lighting a few torches so that the event area was better illuminated. Finally, Julijana was feeling weary after working since dawn on the family's farm, and now beyond dusk at the church. She was pleased to see the young priest coming toward her, for she was certain he would be telling her it was time to quit work for the day.

As he drew closer, she thought he was smiling so she smiled back. He came very close appearing to have a secret to tell her. She held still politely awaiting his words. His message surprised her a bit, but she accepted what the holy man said which was to leave what she was doing and to kindly follow him inside so that he might review the finishing touches to be done in the morning while they, the priests, were conducting Mass. Once inside the priests' residence she was led down a corridor, which appeared to be in the back of the building but overlooking the lake. It was a fairly dark room, a bit reminiscent of a tomb with its construction out of large boulders. The room contained a few cots or daybeds so she wondered if it was a place for resting or meditation, or even a sick room; perhaps it housed another storage closet. It was somewhat cool and damp, and a shiver went through her. She hoped this discussion would be a quick one, or their material could be taken to a more comfortable area, although the view of the lake below was magnificent with its church on the island well lit for the night.

At this point Father said that he did not wish her to be frightened, but that he understood many of the women from the town accepted that the priests suffered under an extremely inhumane burden of celibacy, and they were willing to be charitable and of comfort to them. Further, he had been watching how she moved and how she spoke, and he felt his intimate needs might well be kept a secret, like a sacrament, between the two of them. The room they were in, he explained, was away from everyone; very quiet and very private. Then he asked, "Do you know what I am saying to you?"

With this he stepped quite close to her and dared to take her hand. She could smell the plum wine on his breath and something else, rather musky, that she had occasionally noticed on her brothers, it seemed to arise from inside his clothing. She replied "Father, I think that I do know, but I must ask you not to request this of me, for I am not a woman of the world, but in truth still a girl."

Then the predatory priest smiled widely and said, "Then this will be even more of a sacrament my beautiful virgin." He increased the pressure on her wrist pulling her hand down onto his hardening body and pulling the pins from her hair. She was soon forced to taste that plum wine from his lips and tongue.

8

DREAMS, WORRIES, AND ESCAPES

The priest sprang from the bed at first light and disappeared somewhere down the corridor leading out of the stale, damp, tomb-like chamber in which he had forced himself on poor Julijana. She immediately began pulling her clothing back on, for he had not left her alone all night, although it was possible that she might have dozed off briefly. Now she was exhausted, shaky and almost feverish with anger. Such a man, she thought, with his robes, prayers and duties to God, should not be called a man of God for he is a devil. And she spat on the floor.

She wondered if he immediately went to the older priest and confessed his sins, or did he brag about them? Were the two priests complicit? She felt truly ill at this, and knew her job was both short-lived and over. She would leave an excuse with the housekeeper and make her way home.

As soon as she slipped out of the parish house she began thinking of her mother. She could not bear to tell her dear mother what had happened. Her mother loved the church, and the priests, and leaned hard on her faith to get through these dire times. Justa would pray for a rabbit in the trap, or extra eggs to be left by the chickens, and when it happened, she would offer thanks to God. Julijana would need a compelling reason for quitting this job. Finally, she thought to at least tell part of the truth.

When she arrived home, she said, "Mother please forgive me, but I could not sleep at all last night being so removed from you and the family. It was cold and damp there, and several times Father called for me to bring him something so that I could never fully rest. Now today I feel tired and ill. If I could sleep for but an hour, I am sure I can again be of help to you!" And by this time a sob caught in her throat.

Justa said, "Of course you must rest my dear; I wasn't thinking that you would be home anyway. Sleep all you can, and then come find me."

So Julijana slept a restless sleep of one who feels damned by deep guilt, shame, and anger. She could not forgive herself for allowing this action to have taken place. Then suddenly, she sat straight up as though pushed from under the mattress, and loudly sucked in her breath in a gasp. "What will I do" she stammered, "if I am with child?"

That was when she began to count the days. It seemed she might have been about mid-cycle over the last few days which she knew to be the best time for conception, and the worst time to have had intercourse under these circumstances. The feeling in her heart and gut could only be described as terror. Desperation and hopelessness also entered into it. She must think of what to do in the worst case. Perhaps she would have to fake getting her monthly in order to hedge for more time to plot her next move.

In a house with three menstruating women with no financial means, rags had to be used to absorb their blood, and these rags had to be washed and shared. Typically, when Justa was not pregnant, she would have her cycle begin followed a few days later by Julijana, and then by Mojca. Each woman would take clean rags from a small cupboard used solely for this purpose. When they had been used, she would rinse them at the pump, and then leave them soaking in a bucket behind the house. The next woman to need the rags would take what she required, and then wring out the soaking rags, and see that they dried in time for the next person, or her own use, depending upon the requirements of her body. This could go on for several days per woman so that clean rags were a precious commodity. It was very bad behavior to complete your need without checking to be certain all rags were being dried. These women would have been amazed to think of a culture so wealthy and decadent that women only used new material, and disposed of it after each use.

These thoughts helped Julijana to find a plan for concealing her problem, should she have one. On the day her cycle was due to start, she would take rags from the cupboard. A few hours later she would rinse and then soak them, going through the whole process until she would have logically had no more need for such things. At least her mother would not be alerted before Julijana could determine what to do. And whether it was fear, trauma, or an actual conception, she was convinced of her pregnancy less than a week after her cycle was late. For some clocklike women, that is enough time to know.

Her thought was to get help from the priest. He had done this to her; he must get her into hiding so that she might have the baby away from her home - and save them all disgrace and more hardship. She had never planned to go to that church again, never wanted to see Father's smiling face, or hear of his urgent problem, but she would have to find the courage to walk into the church. And so, as she knew the schedule for confession she walked up to the church and got in line hoping the older priest was not on duty that day.

Soon it was her turn in the confessional. She was behind a partition and could not know who was on the other side. She sat and recited "Bless me father for I have sinned."

He replied, "And what is the nature of your sin?"

To which she said, "I allowed an older and powerful man to force me into fornication and now believe that I am pregnant." Julijana was fighting back tears as she said these words, but she was determined to be forthright and strike an undeniable blow. She also knew she could not spare the true situation if she hoped to receive any help.

There was an audible sigh from the priest's side of the booth. Then he began in a soft voice saying "You must make an act of contrition and say the rosary. And so must I. What are your thoughts about what must be done, and does anyone else know of this issue?"

"I alone, and now you, know of this. I wish to leave the area and have the baby far away so that my family is not touched by disgrace. I ask you for enough money to get me to Vienna on the train, and a few weeks of food and lodging while I find work. Then you will never hear from me again."

He replied with not more apologizing but went straight to the easy out she had given him. "Yes," he said, "Please meet me at the backdoor of the parish house at seven PM on Saturday. Mass will be over, and I will be there with what you need." Then he added "And I will pray for you."

While there was no 'dream come true' for poor Julijana, she at least felt that she had done what had to be done, and would obtain what she needed, to have a chance of making a life for herself and the baby. Although deep down she knew that there was not enough money for families to survive, so the chances for a woman alone with a baby would be most difficult. But being young and not truly aware of what the world was really like proved to be an advantage allowing her to move forward.

Once the money was in her hands, she told her mother that she must leave and make her own way in the world; that Rositha and Vilma were already big enough to be of help and not burdens; and that leaving would make more room for the others, although she loved them all. It was difficult, especially for Justa to let go of her beautiful first-born daughter, but she slowly accepted it along with promises from Julijana of visits home as soon as possible.

She had not many things to pack. Her two brothers walked her to the train station so that she would be safe and not unaccompanied. They were too poor to have a wagon for her use, but the train station was just a little farther away than the church. As she stepped up to board the train, Andrej Jr. handed her a note. He said it was from their mother. They all looked perplexed because Justa generally had great difficulty in writing, but there must have been something she needed to say.

Andrej and Ivan wished her well. They also handed her the food their mother had packed, reminded her to write to them, ending with an admonishment to her not to read the note until the train had pulled out of the station, for that was their mother's request.

9

LEAVING HOME BY TRAIN

Julijana spent a few minutes attempting to become oriented to what was expected of her on a train. Where did one sit, how would her ticket be collected, and did she need to place her bag in the rack above her seat, or directly under her? She tried to do as she saw others do; even figuring out that they placed their tickets within a little bar on the back of the seat in front of them. The next thing she wanted was to see her brothers through the window so that she could wave to them one more time. Alas, the grime on both the inside and the outside of the glass was too thick for her to have a clear view; nor, she reasoned, would they be able to see her. With a heavy sigh she sat semi-straddling her bag, not far from where she had entered the train.

The smell of the train's steamy discharge filled the air, along with bits of cinders. She had even seen sparks glowing in the outside air and then landing as hard black bits. Suddenly, everything started to shake and move in such a manner she feared that the train would soon disintegrate into a heap of metal, wood, and seat cushions. Then there was a powerful lurch, and the entire train screeched forward to begin what eventually became a monotonous shaking and twisting. As the car rolled through towns, she would see some of the sights, despite the grime, and was looking forward to what the mountains might look like up close, but she felt uneasy with all the motion, noise and smell.

Then she felt a little hungry, and remembered the food her mother had packed for her, and the letter. Inside the cloth in which her food was wrapped she found cheese, a large portion of sausage, a quarter of a loaf of bread, and an apple. It was far too generous; Julijana was immediately filled with guilt to have taken this food from the family, knowing full well her mother must be going without that night, sacrificing for her. She ate a little, and decided to make the rest last, for she had no idea from where her next meal would come. She stowed the wrapper and contents into the side of her bag. Then she picked up the note.

The note bore but a few words: *The water not pink. I love you, mamma.*

Julijana whispered these words to herself to try and understand them. Then her eyes filled with tears. Her mother knew she was pregnant! "The water not pink," of course, when her mother had gone to wring out the rags before drying, she had found them too clean. The soaking in the pail, which was meant to release the last little bit of blood, of which there was always some remaining, had produced very clear water – too clear for her daughter to have really been using them as they typically were. Justa knew her secret and had allowed her to solve the problem as best she could. Yet, she still declared that she loved Julijana.

"Oh, mamma," she sighed, "I will find a way back to you, and I shall always love you too."

With that she cried herself to sleep awaking only occasionally when there was a sudden change in motion, or when the train passed through a tunnel, and the engineer sounded the whistle. She had heard that sound every day from her home on the hill, but it was much louder from within the train. Finally, the train made its descent from the mountains gaining ground into Austria with the lights of Vienna actually visible in the distance far ahead.

Shortly, she would arrive in Vienna with a little money, a little food, no friends or even contacts, and a baby growing in her belly. Inside her head she thought "I will do this one step at a time. First, I must find lodging, and then I must acquire work that will provide enough money to cover my costs until I am able to figure more out. Finding a friend or two would also be a good idea, she added, as she now felt utterly lonely. It was as though she had gone to sleep a child and had now awakened staring into the abyss of adulthood which seemed like stepping off the highest peak of the Alps into thin air with pointed rocks below gleaming at her. No mother, father, sisters or brothers to buffer her leap; she would manage her life as an adult or fall to her death trying.

Julijana stepped carefully from the train. Her legs continued to vibrate from the trip, although perhaps the vibrations were in her head; for certain she felt dizzy but made her way from the station, crossed the street, and asked a woman who was selling fruit from a cart if she knew where there were rooms to rent. The woman had looked like another farmer to her with sweat-stained clothing and a dirty apron tied about her. She took this to be someone whom she could approach for help. But this woman was not interested in her and brusquely said, "No." The farm woman continued to call out for anyone who wanted ripe apples, pears, and grapes.

Feeling even more shaken she continued to walk as though with purpose, as if she knew the city, until at a corner she could smell coffee, and knew she must be at a café. She took a seat within this shop, but as near to the door as possible in case she wished to exit hurriedly, already fearing she would be rebuffed as had just occurred. A man wearing a clean apron approached her and asked what she wanted. He was robust giving the impression that he owned this business and was doing well.

She replied, "A cup of coffee please."

He replied, "And a sweet bun?"

"How much are your rolls?" she asked. Then demurred when he spoke the amount, for she had such a precious small amount to last her for an undefined time.

When he came back with the coffee, there was a sticky bun sitting next to it on a little doily along with a cloth napkin. "Oh," she cried out, "I cannot afford this right now!"

To which the waiter remarked, "The man with the newspaper in the front window asked that I give this to you. It is he who has paid for it, the coffee too." And he left.

She smiled nervously and glanced his way, but he continued as if engrossed in his paper. She found the coffee and the confection both delectable; surprising herself with the enthusiasm with which she consumed it given she had not felt well for several mornings of late. Then the gentleman got up and walked toward her, or perhaps toward the exit next to her.

When he stopped at her table, she spoke up thanking him for the kind gift. He had a very German way of speaking, but she supposed that was how it would be in Austria. She could understand him well enough from her experience with the tourists who had been in their part of the world. He said "Happy to help someone new to Vienna, Fraulein. Is there anything more I may do for you?"

Even after riding all night on a train, crying herself to sleep, and not feeling fresh or presentable, her beauty was sufficient to entice one of the first people she met to offer her help.

"I would be so grateful if you could direct me to a boarding house for respectable young ladies," she said in German; it was a phrase which she had rehearsed in anticipation of making this request.

Then he answered her in Slovenian with barely a trace of an accent as he must have clearly detected from where her accent originated. "There is a place three corners from here. If you come now, I will walk you to it directly. And please, may I carry your bag?"

She had been warned that there were bad men everywhere and not to trust any strangers. But since it was broad daylight, and they would be walking on a public way, she accepted. Being tired and afraid of further inquiries probably also softened her judgment, but she truly needed a place to rest before she could do anything further. They walked a few feet apart around busy street corners filled with people, tall buildings, fast moving horses and an occasional automobile. It felt like a magical kingdom from one of her childhood books. She was almost giddy with combined exhaustion and excitement when they reached the stark, three-story, brick building which was the boarding house.

The gentleman, who had given his name as Fritz, told her to meet him at the same coffee house that evening for a bowl of soup and so that he might find out what else she needed. She thanked him and entered her new home.

10

MAKING A NEW FRIEND

She slept as though there were no worries in the world, then awakened with a start at the realization that she was in a strange bed, in a strange setting, and in a city which here-to-for had only been a name to her. Vienna, the beautiful city of music, art, and the monarchy; here I am to greet you. The architecture and height of the buildings had amazed her on the walk over earlier in the day. Why, she had wondered, were there so many buildings so close together?

Gazing out her window she studied the street before returning to examine the room. There appeared to be a stable up at the corner to her right, then a butcher (perhaps if the horses would not behave, she joked to herself), then two sets of doors leading up to apartment buildings directly across from her. These were made of wood and appeared to be rather old, and a bit shabby. It was difficult to see what lay beyond her window, although she had certainly observed some of it when she entered the boarding house as guided by Mr. Fritz.

The first thing she observed was that her room was clean, for which she was grateful, having heard tales, when in school, of rats carrying fleas with diseases. Of course, that was many years ago within harbor cities, and then it spread throughout the country. The room itself contained a small bed with a canopy. The quilt was a rather dull blue, perhaps from being washed many times, and did not match the white above the bed. There was a stand with a basin, and a pitcher of water. She hastened to the pitcher which had a blue floral etching on its porcelain front.

Julijana decide to go to the water closet first, which was three doors down the hall, and then to freshen up for her meeting later that afternoon. She had one other dress in her bag which she hoped to fluff out from its travel wrinkles. She also had undergarments, the nightdress she had worn at the church, and an apron should the work she might find require protection. While washing herself she decided she would spot clean the dress she had worn on the train and rinse out her under-things so that she would not be caught without clean clothes. Only two dresses, and no sister from whom to borrow, left her a bit anxious about keeping herself looking decent.

Dressed in fresh garments, and with her cleaned items drying in the little closet she had found in her room, she headed off for a slow walk to the café. She wished to begin memorizing what was located on this street, and to see if there were any "Help Wanted" signs in the shop windows. The café looked smaller to her as she entered it this time, perhaps she was a little less overwhelmed by everything, and there was Mr. Fritz sitting in a corner. He rose when she approached him, and he grinned rather broadly seeing that she had kept her word to meet him.

He began by telling her how good the Wiener schnitzel was, or perhaps she would like the beef barley soup? Having little idea how one behaves in a restaurant, and not wishing to lose her only friend, she replied, "I will have whatever the gentleman is having."

And so, they began a rather awkward conversation about who he was, and what she wanted to find in Vienna. He told her he was an artist. She asked, "Do you paint great works of art that hang in galleries?"

To which he replied, "Sometimes they hang in galleries, but mostly in the homes of the wealthy. I paint portraits, dogs, children, horses and estates; whatever someone wants to pay me to paint. That is how I earn a living, on these commissions."

"Oh," she said, "That sounds very glamorous. I need work but I'm afraid I've only held a brush to help paint the barn."

He laughed at that. "Well," he added, "I could use a helper in my shop as business is good. How would you feel about picking up my supplies, cleaning my brushes, and sweeping out the shop plus scheduling the customers who want portraits painted?"

"But you know so little about me. Are you certain you want to hire me so quickly?"

"Well," he said, "I am certain you are a good Catholic girl and would never rob your employer."

At the mention of "Catholic" she was reminded of her condition, due to the unholy priest, and she blushed to a fuchsia color. He asked if he had said the wrong thing and she assured him that he had not. She would be honored to take the job if it was within walking distance of her boarding house.

He suggested they walk to the shop after their meal so she could then better judge the distance. They arrived at a sublevel business that did have windows reaching up from the ground. Although one entered by a door at the bottom of four steps, the building was set back a few paces, allowing air and light to rest on the front windows which were below street level. These windows were easily eight feet high and twelve feet wide. Once inside the shop, the light diminished with each step one took, but Fritz had gaslighting to illuminate what he needed if he worked late, or the day was dreary.

There were several easels in the room, a large sink filled with brushes, many discarded clothes or rags with paint on them, and several boxes of small paint tins which he used to mix on his pallets to make the desired shades. He told Julijana that he would teach her how to prepare the colors he used frequently, so that he would save time. There was also a couch, of sorts, on a raised dais, with a light- weight blanket draped over its back. He told her that was where his models posed so that maximum light would fall on them.

She didn't know what to say, so he began questioning her. "How much will you need to be paid to make ends meet? Because I will give you raises, but first I must see how you perform."

"Well," she began, "They charge me four krone a day for the room, use of the facilities, plus coffee and a biscuit. The landlady said sometimes there could be cheese too."

He made a whistling sound. "If you add that all up, times the days in a month, you won't have money for other meals, clothing and any basic necessities you might require with the salary I was to offer you. Let me think."

He then jumped up as though suddenly struck by a jet of his gas complete with flame, and exclaimed, "Why didn't I think of this sooner? When I first opened this shop I didn't have enough money to pay rent here, and on an apartment, so I turned the back storage room into sort of a bedroom and have really never reclaimed it for storage. There's a cot, a two-burner gas stove top, no oven, mind you, but an icebox that holds the cold pretty well. There's also this large sink right here, and a toilet just down the hall. We share it with the haberdasher next door – why it's hardly used by him! If you start the coffee each morning before I arrive, I'll count us even for the use of the space. Just be advised that sometimes a shy model will want to undress back there, so you'll have to be prepared to share it for a few hours, and NEVER leave any valuables about."

She blushed at this, knowing she had no valuables to be leaving out, and at the thought of naked people posing in the same room in which she would be working. "I paid the landlady for the next four days. Shall I move in right after that?"

And Fritz smiled, "Why, yes, my dear. That will be just fine."

11

THOSE WHO REMAINED

Mojca felt the absence of her sister even though her first thought had been "Finally a room of my own!" In her entire life she had hardly known a day without Julijana in it. The first night alone she had attempted to read in bed since there was no one to disturb with her lamp burning longer, but in mere moments she was daydreaming more about what her sister might be doing than she was concentrating on her book. She was a bit jealous of Julijana's freedom and adventure; and more than a little concerned for how she would manage in a city bigger than anything they had ever seen. The people she had met from Vienna, while helping with the pletna, were certainly pleasant, and often tipped them well. But that raised another issue. How was her sister acquiring the funds she would need for rent and food? Perhaps she would find a group of other young women seeking to share an apartment.

If Julijana had an apartment, would she welcome Mojca as a visitor? That could be great fun she thought, but then realized that the expense of travel, when the family was barely able to find enough food to subsist, left this idea beyond reach. Additionally, their mother seemed particularly sad without her oldest daughter. Mojca didn't want to add to her distress or loneliness. She rushed around the house each morning hoping to get ahead of the chores her sister usually performed, and then rushed down the hill to see what was needed with the boats.

The pletna had been less in demand since the Great War; and some of this was related to the fact that Slovenia was now part of the Kingdom of Serbs, Croats and Slovenes under the leadership of King Peter I. He had been the King of Serbia, but now, supposedly led them all, which caused bitter feelings, and cut down on the passion of pilgrims to travel to the Assumption of Maria church which was not well thought of by the Serbs. Further, the church was named for Maria Theresa of Austria, and they were no longer part of Austria-Hungary. For those born well before the Great War, it seemed as if the world were confused. They were in a game where no one knew the rules, but they could be in trouble without really understanding why.

Several weeks went by with Mojca simply keeping herself busy trying not to think about her sister or Julijana's life. The emptiness left by her sister's absence could not be filled with any of her chores. Then one morning she and her father arrived early at the dock to find an awning slashed and terrible words written on the boats. In addition, much of their gear, which was used to tie the boats, or row them, lay strewn about the lawn. A beautiful swan which had floated gently by each day was beaten to death on the edge of the lake. Andrej, Sr. and Mojca were at first speechless, and then both father and daughter used Slovenian words that would have caused the sun to blister, so disgusted were they with the senseless damage done to their boats, and the cruel death of a magnificent and helpless creature.

Due to the destruction of that night, many hours of work and some expense was created for the family. Mojca decided that the pletna could no longer be left alone in the dark. She thought of bringing a mean dog to live on the boats, but feared these intruders might shoot it, so she discussed it with Andrej junior. Yes, he thought, guard duty was a fine idea. Shortly before dark each evening, he and Mojca would set up camp at the boat site. They built a fire on the lawn for a little cheer and warmth. They also thought that the fire would warn troublemakers away as they would know there were people on duty; perhaps thinking it might be men rather than an eighteen-year-old girl and her sixteen-year-old brother armed only with a wooden pistol. And for many months they had no further trouble.

Then, one early spring evening in 1921, they arrived late having eaten at home rather than bringing a picnic type meal to eat on the boats. It was really too late to build the fire, so they just pulled their bedding out from under the boats' seats and settled in for the night. Perhaps two hours or more had passed. Then they were awakened by distant ribald laughter headed their way. They crouched down behind their seats, each in a different boat, each armed with a few stones. The voices grew louder and they heard planning going on for the boarding of the boats and an apparent launch. These four fellows wanted to go over to the church and desecrate it before coming back to the landing and destroying the boats.

As they reached Mojca's pletna she struck two on the legs with rocks thrown with great force. Each boy cried out as though he had been shot. She then stood and said, "I will use worse than rocks should you come any further!"

The boys were quiet for a moment and then began to laugh as though it was the greatest of jokes "Look it's only a girl!" They were bending over at the waist really having a good hearty laugh.

Then, out of the darkness came a much deeper voice, for Andrej Jr.'s voice had already changed. "Yes, only a girl and her armed body-guard!" he said. With that he stood up on the seat of the pletna, which added a foot to his height. The moon was in just the right direction to outline him in silhouette. And that black figure showed a man brandishing a gun held in a military stance with two hands.

To say that the boys left hurriedly would be an understatement. They virtually flew across the lawn, for a moment appearing to almost jump in the lake, but they thought better of that and took off around the curves of the lawn, and headed up an alley between shops across from the water. They could be heard yelling, "Keep running!" as they departed.

Mojca and Andrej collapsed together in her boat laughing. Then she cautioned, "It really isn't funny. Next time they may come back and bring a gun of their own, possibly a real gun!"

Andrej replied, "Perhaps it is time for your bodyguard to bear arms himself."

The memory of this night worried Mojca. She was sure that not only her pretty boats would be ruined by these wild boys, but possibly her brother would be injured as well. She continued to guard the business with him, but her attitude about the pletna and her life as defined by a future with the boats was no longer tantalizing to her. She might just as well be shoveling coal at the train station as protecting these now tarnished vessels.

Andrej had a different reaction to that night. He did, in fact, arm himself with a real weapon and taught himself to shoot without flinching from the recoil. His aim was true. He had acquired the gun by talking to the police in Ljubljana. He had ridden there by train and told the constable their story of stopping the pletna and church destruction. The officers were amused, and decided to deputize this young man to act with authority at Lake Bled. They thought there might be other assignments he could take on for them once this was resolved. Andrej pledged his allegiance to the police and promised to act on the King's behalf for justice. It would not be too many more months before he would qualify to officially apply for and attain a job with the Royal Army of Yugoslavia. He was certain this was what he wanted to do, for while he could never bring himself to harm an innocent animal, he had come to understand that there was evil intent in man.

When he explained this all to Mojca, she didn't respond as he had expected. Mojca felt even more determined to try some other kind of life, as the peace and beauty she had so cherished here was totally undermined, especially as her baby brother was now a policeman in training. She disliked guns, violence, and the rage that went with it. Somewhere, she thought, there must be an area where fighting is not either just beginning, just ending, or people are plotting for revenge or control.

A few weeks after she became determined to change her life, a young man began what immediately seemed like a flirtation with Mojca. They had met as he had been accompanying a group traveling over to the church by boat. He told her he would be back with another group the following week. Could she arrange to be there again?

His name was Vid, and he was a Slovenian living in Vienna since his parents left before the Great War. He was very tall and loved to row boats. He was also handsome, charming, and had a wonderful sense of humor. He often came with various groups as a guide and interpreter given that he spoke five languages fluently. The next time he came he asked Mojca to go with them back to Vienna. She said she would meet him there and stay with her sister once she had acquired a ticket.

The following morning, when she stepped from her house, there was an envelope with her name on it sitting on a post and held down by a rock. The ticket inside this envelope was all that she needed to become the second child to leave home. She had heard from Julijana just twice. Once was to say she was well and had married an artist, the next stated that they were the proud parents of a baby boy named Peter Andrej Fritz. A German, Mojca thought I would not have expected that.

PART THREE

THE DISTANT SOUND
OF PLANES

12

BECOMING A CITIZEN
OF THE WORLD

Immediately, when Mojca arrived in Vienna, she contacted Julijana for their first reunion in what was now four years. Mojca was asked to meet them at Mr. Fritz's studio where both the Fritzes worked during the day, and at which little Peter was expected to play quietly in a corner. Mojca had to admit that she walked right by the door on her first pass through the street, but then realized that the studio was down a short flight of stairs. Here, she finally saw Julijana again and hugged her handsome nephew.

The father was working with a client, and only glanced briefly toward Mojca, but he seemed pleased to meet her by the way he bowed slightly toward her, and there was warmth in his smile. Mojca thought he looked too old for her sister, and then dismissed the thought as none of her business, yet she could not avoid the strong sense that Peter looked nothing like his dad. If Julijana had a story to tell she would wait to hear it, not presume to criticize or suggest fault. So, this first reunion was filled with laughter, tears and the joy of playing with Peter.

Near evening Mojca made excuses to return to her hotel. She did say that the friend she had met in Slovenia would be coming to take her to dinner. She did not mention that he would also be spending the night with her. Mojca was very excited to have this chance to actually be in bed with her lover instead of leaning on a side wall of the boathouse, or up against a tree on the edge of the woods. She did not know if she wanted to marry Vid, but she did want to be with him, wherever he might go. Her hope was that they should eventually find their way to a peaceful country, even if that meant leaving Slovenia, and now Austria, behind.

But those were future thoughts. They were both invited to Julijana's and her husband Hansi Fritz's, home for dinner the next night. They found the small, one bedroom apartment, on the second floor of a townhouse building about three blocks from the studio. This apartment shared a bathroom with the apartment right above it. For the Fritzes it was a luxury, as they had only to step into the hall for access, but the other folks had also to walk down a flight of stairs. The Fritzes' apartment had a pretty lavender shade, of what looked like ribbon, running through the wallpaper with white lacey curtains in both the living room and the small dining room. The boy's bed was in one corner of this dining room so getting the chairs around the table was tight. Then the couple had a bedroom with one window and small flowered wallpaper in the same shade of lavender as the ribbon print. The kitchen, also small, was half taken up by the gas oven and was painted white with a few checkered tiles on the floor.

After considerable wine, Julijana told the story of her arrival in Vienna more than four years ago. She said, "I arrived with very little money and part of a lunch my mother had packed for me. With advice from Hansi," she said smiling lovingly at him and patting his hand, "I found temporary accommodations in a boardinghouse for respectable women, then met Hansi later that day where he offered me a job and a cot in the back storage room."

Apparently, Mojca opened her eyes very wide at this story prompting Julijana to add, "The cot wasn't as bad as it might sound, and I could even cook in the studio; all without charge."

"But the first morning I came into work was the first day that I experienced morning sickness, and there was no hiding it as I had to keep running to the sink, pushing brushes aside, and retching! Poor Hansi didn't know what to say. He couldn't bring himself to ask me anything, or to fire me, so he let it go on for several days."

"Finally, it was the day I was to move from the boardinghouse to the shop, and Hansi insisted on coming with me to help with anything heavy. Although I barely possessed a thing, it was nice to have his company. Then he insisted on carrying the one lamp I had bought, as well as the suitcase, saying it wasn't good for me to lift much in my condition."

"Then I knew my secret could no longer be contained. I broke down and told him everything, expecting full well to be fired. Instead, later that same night, he proposed to me. I was overjoyed to find such a good man and one who promised to raise the baby as his own. Not many men would do that."

Hansi interrupted, "Such a beautiful and brave woman, it was I who received a prize, with a prize inside." And he laughed loudly as though this quite pleased him.

After congratulations Mojca felt that she would burst if she did not ask her question. "Then who, pray tell, is the baby's father?"

Julijana said, "I will tell you, but this information shall not go back home. Agreed?" she asked, while scanning the room. Then she told of her night in the priests' house, and a bit about what the younger priest had done, enough so that there was no mistaking the act had been sufficient to result in the dear little boy who played near the table.

Mojca asked, "Does mother know?"

"She figured out that I was pregnant, but I would rather not come between her and her love of God. Perhaps she suspects the priest yet never asked. Tell me, does she still go to church?"

"Yes," Mojca said, "Maybe more than ever with Andrej Jr. in the service of the Royal Army carrying a gun. She prays for him to be safe and to always act with wisdom."

"Such a good mother," replied Julijana, then, "What of Ivan?"

"Well," said Mojca, "Since Andrej began working for the King, Ivan has talked nonstop of becoming a railroad man. I suppose he sees this as nearly as masculine as being an armed guard and he has always loved the trains. Papa seems troubled that no one wants to be a farmer after he has spent his life acquiring good land and expanding it bit by bit. But Ivan clearly wants something different with a regular paycheck and a chance to see different places. Perhaps Rositha or Vilma will marry farmers and keep the farm going; although honestly I doubt it. Rositha loves school, so maybe she will be a teacher."

Then the conversation switched to what was the next step for Mojca and her friend Vid. Mojca thought they might stay in Austria for a while, and then perhaps return to Slovenia to be company for Justa and Papa. Maybe, one day to take over the pletna if no one else had accepted this duty as she still loved the boats and the lake. Vid said he would be willing to return to Slovenia too if there was any future for him in his homeland. The politics were always in turmoil, and that made planning so difficult. They would be waiting to see what happened next. There was always fighting somewhere in this Kingdom of Serbs, Croats and Slovenes. Vid was beginning to think they should move to Australia although, at this time, he dared not mention it out loud to Mojca.

Julijana sighed as she heard these things. "Yes," she said, "I would like to take little Peter to meet his grandparents and to play with the sheep on the farm; and to have everyone meet my wonderful husband" and she winked at Hansi, "But not if trouble could erupt again while we were away from Austria. We feel safer here."

With that, the party seemed to break-up for the evening. It was getting late for Peter to stay up, and Julijana and Hansi would have dinner dishes to wash even though Mojca and Vid had offered several times to help. The meal had been lovely and most appreciated by the travelers. It consisted of freshly made hard crusted bread with a little oil beside it, followed by sausage cooked with cabbage, rice and garden carrots. Obviously, the Fritzes had given all that they could provide that evening. All over Europe, families continued to struggle following the Great War, and only those who might work for the wealthy, such as Hansi as an artist, had any assurances of some money coming in. It was hard times everywhere with fears of the future. This is probably why Julijana could not trust that it would be wise to visit home anytime soon. More time was needed to heal these countries, and faith had to be built that the trouble was really over, if, indeed, it was.

13

CHANGING OF THE KINGS

In 1921, the year before Mojca and Vid arrived in Vienna, Peter I, head of the Kingdom of Serbs, Croats and Slovenes passed away, leaving his son Alexander, who was serving as Regent, to lead the Kingdom. He became known as Alexander the Unifier and went from being Prince Regent, eventually to King of Yugoslavia, until 1934 when he was assassinated in Marseille, France. This left Alexander's eleven-year-old son, as Peter II, King of Yugoslavia. His cousin Paul would act as regent until, at age seventeen, Peter II was declared of age in a coup, and served as the last King of Yugoslavia, deposed in 1941 and becoming King in Exile as WWII had begun in earnest.

The people of Eastern Europe continued to suffer from instabilities in their governments, with a paucity of food and commerce. Fascist groups were organizing, gaining power, and taking control of various countries. Benito Mussolini led Italy with deadly force through labor organizations until he became Prime Minister. Generalisimo Francisco Franco led the Nationalist Forces in overthrowing the Spanish Republic and remained as dictator from 1939 to 1975.

Adolf Hitler was Fuhrer and chancellor of Germany attaining this power through his leadership of the Nazi Party beginning in the early 1920s. And the Balkan countries had been at war off and on for decades prior to The Great War. It is easier for these militaristic, dictatorial regimes to attain power when people are hungry and poor; the populace becomes willing to cleave to any powerful force claiming that their lives will be improved. And in the case of the Nazis, the followers are more susceptible to blaming others for their plights if their bellies are not full. This grave unrest did not yet reflect the atrocities which would kill six million Jews and erupt into heavy fighting across Europe as well as the Mediterranean and Middle East.

Julijana, Hansi, Peter, Mojca and Vid remained in Vienna during many of these upheavals. There was an ever-increasing sense that another major war was coming, but in many ways the signs were subtle yet growing steadily. Much of the tension beyond the borders of Austria and Yugoslavia was coming from Germany. Its chancellor was busy raising taxes on all businesses while demanding membership in Aryan clubs for school children, as long as they were of nearly pure German blood. Hitler believed Austria was a part of Germany. After all, he had been born in Austria, and the citizens of both countries spoke German.

German businessmen who traveled by train into Yugoslavia during this period would complain of the money Hitler demanded from their companies, and therefore the decreasing margin of profit. Those in manufacturing also stated that they were being required to change their production lines. That is, if they had been making car parts, they were now being told to convert to making similar parts for tanks and perhaps planes. Many of these changes involved incredible costs at the manufacturer's expense yet they did not dare to overtly complain or decline to do as they were told. To anyone who would listen, the sound of marching was growing louder and resounding over the mountain tops. It was the vibration of thousands of marching feet, the hum and buzz of airplane engines, and the rumble of tanks making the earth quake; but worse than all of these noises was the screaming of civilians and soldiers as they died with no comprehension of why they must, and who could possibly benefit from their demise.

In the early thirties, Vid began insisting that they all get out of Austria. He was smart, still traveled, and could hear that marching, perhaps ahead of others. But Hansi had once met Adolf Hitler, who also fancied himself a painter, and the two men had bonded over art. Hansi suspected that he could play a role in a new government if it ever came to pass. He had started attending Nazi party meetings and believed he could protect his family in this way if things ever came to war. Whenever Julijana mentioned the possibility of leaving Austria with her sister, he urged her to visit her family in Slovenia, but to hurry home afterwards.

And so, in 1937, Julijana and Peter would make their last visit to the farm where his grandparents lived with their three youngest children. While she was home, Julijana would learn that both Rositha and Vilma were planning to leave for England. They wanted to have more of a life than the farm could offer them. They had enough of eating porridge and having to forage for berries; of meeting men who were increasingly more polarized toward one faction or another but definitely anxious to go to war; they disliked the marching sounds coming over the mountains and much preferred the thinking of those in England. They had saved their money and were leaving for

England as soon as this visit was over with its brief celebration of their brother's wedding.

Andrej Jr. had waited until he had been able to save a little of his pay before he took over a small farmhouse in need of repairs near Belgrade on the edge of his wife's hometown. He was thirty-years-old and ready to be a husband and run his own home. He was a fulltime, armed member, of the Royal Army of Yugoslavia and proud to serve in this way. He felt it a noble calling to protect the King's laws and citizens.

His bride was a girl who was as pretty as a movie star, sweet and religious like his mother. Her name was Marica and she thought him a hero because he was in the Royal Army. She loved to cook and make clothing. About the only thing she had ever done wrong was, prior to the marriage, allowing Andrej to touch her in places she should not have. But even that stopped short of losing her virginity, so she wore her white lace wedding gown with pride. That dress would soon be curtains in their new home.

They were married in the city with all her family in attendance in a large church. His parents could not make the difficult journey to Belgrade. The trip they made now was so that his parents could relive the wedding in the smaller church near their farm, the one surrounded by a village, rather than the grander church overlooking the lake. This church, too, was beautiful, with a high steeple and lofty ceiling, and much easier for many people to walk to for the service. They had a modest reception in the rectory following the ceremony, as no one could afford to give away much food in any celebration during these times. Still, there was plum wine, beer, bowls of goulash, and small honey cakes; no one would go hungry.

His sisters, he liked to say, had come from a great distance to honor him, as he thought of Mojca and Julijana traveling from Vienna;

and his youngest two sisters had postponed their world travel to also be present for this auspicious day. They had missed the original wedding, but this little wedding was also a family reunion. It was a little more difficult to describe Ivan's behavior that day.

Ivan had gone to work for the railroad just as soon as he was old enough to qualify. But, less than six months before this wedding, he had been involved in an accident that nearly took his life. He was helping the engineer to fill the furnace with coal which would generate the steam needed to move the train, when something mixed in with the coal exploded as it hit the fire, sending a large chunk of metal into the side of his head. He was not expected to live.

Ivan was transferred to Ljubljana to a medical school hospital where the surgeon replaced some of his shattered skull with a metal plate. They told his parents that they had removed all foreign particles from his brain including fragments of his own bone. When he was eventually sent home, the railroad taking care of all expenses and transportation, it was with strict instructions not to move his head for the next six months unless absolutely necessary; not to get overly excited by anything; and not to drink. He was able to live up to the first two and had improved. He could speak again, and that was the most critical thing, and he could walk, albeit slowly, in order to comply with not moving his head too much. But he was no longer exactly the same man as he had once been. They would probably never hunt again, and certainly not drag a large buck out of the forest, nor were they likely to roughhouse or arm wrestle. He was somewhat reserved now and not as full of life. Still, he too attended the wedding, and wished his brother good cheer.

Perhaps they all recognized this as the last opportunity for the six children and their parents to ever be together. A war was coming;

the oldest two girls already lived in another country, and the youngest two were packed and ticketed to move to London. Surely these young men would be impacted directly by the war; perhaps all of them would be. It was impossible to know, at this point, and if they could have known, they might have chosen to remain ignorant as all their lives would be forever changed.

On March 12, 1938, German troops would march into Austria to claim this nation for Germany and the Third Reich. Of course, there was resistance. Before the war was over, Vienna would be bombed fifty-two times and 37,000 homes would be destroyed. And back on the farm, Justa would die less than a year after Austria was invaded. She would die from years of hard work, bearing six children, a prolonged starvation diet, and the sheer terror of wondering what was happening to her family in Austria, in England and in parts unknown, for her son Andrej was often in harm's way and her daughter Morja was somewhere else, supposedly safe, with Vid.

14

WHERE COULD ONE FIND SAFETY

Rositha was now a grown woman. She had soft brown hair, which she kept at shoulder length or tied in a loose bun, and a trim, athletic figure from a lifetime of hard work. She had also completed all of the education which was offered to her, making it possible for her to become a teacher, although the times were so challenging that no positions were available. When her brother got married in 1937, Rositha was twenty-five years old and prepared to leave for London as soon as the event was over. She'd just help at their farm until things were "back to normal." She wanted to see her sisters off, with the exception of Vilma who would travel with her, as she did not know when she would see any of them again.

Rositha was always reading, and what she gleaned about the actions of the Nazi party frightened her. She studied the thinking of all the countries which would become the Axis of WWII versus the writings of those that represented the thoughts of the Allied Nations. She had also taught herself English watching British and American films, and this further influenced her leaning toward the

Allies. It was her strong opinion that they should all move to the United Kingdom, but only Vilma would listen to her.

It wasn't that her brothers didn't hear her words of caution; they simply had their own lives and plans which remained centered on Slovenia and Belgrade, or all of Yugoslavia. Ivan had a pension from the railroad, and Andrej had just married Marica who certainly would not want to leave Belgrade and her family; nor he his post in the King's Army. As for her parents, they owned land, the pletna rights, and were physically slowing down enough that to start anew in a country where they could not speak the language would be overwhelming. Also, Rositha could not guarantee that they would all be safe in England, only that they could trust the government to be doing what was right for her citizens and humankind.

A few weeks after the wedding, and with many hugs and tears, the two youngest Lovrenc girls left home by train headed for France. In France they would take a short boat ride across the English Channel to the Straights of Dover, and then another train trip into the heart of London where they hoped to start a new life. Yugoslavia had issued them passports and the United Kingdom required no visa.

They were glad to have each other as they arrived at the English Channel. It was huge in the eyes of two country girls who had previously only seen Slovenian lakes. Boarding a ferryboat that also held produce, livestock, and a few automobiles seemed very grand. They had each packed their bicycles with satchels on the back, a filled basket on the front, and small bags hanging from each handlebar. It wasn't easy to peddle bikes packed in this manner, nor did they look like sophisticated travelers, but it did provide them a mode of transportation since they were not sure how they would get around once they arrived in London, and Rositha thought she might even work as a courier if necessary.

They didn't know which way to turn, or to look, once they had disembarked the train in London. Across from the terminal there were carriages pulled by horses fancier than anything the girls had ever seen, meeting ladies who were traveling with servants. These ladies must regularly travel to Paris for shopping from the appearance of their garment bags tied with string and ribbon. Nearly everything they had appeared to have been prepared as a gift, not simply packaged for travel.

The clothing on these women, and even their help, seemed extraordinarily rich. Rositha leaned over and spoke discreetly into Vilma's ear, "There's a job for you, you can wrap M'ladies goods so that she receives presents from herself!" and they both giggled.

But the giggles only thinly concealed how nervous they were, for the crowds and the goods in this area were truly a spectacle to them. They had never seen porters, prams, limousines, and people dressed as servants except in the movies. The streets were all cobblestones and made a great clatter as the horses clopped along them. But the horse droppings also added to the confusion of walking in the streets.

There was something else happening at the terminal; Rositha and Vilma were not the only refugees fleeing the impending war. There were people from many countries steadily making their way into London hoping to avoid horrible catastrophes in their homelands and already suffering from a lack of nutrition. The problem, of course, would be that many who had the most to lose would not realize it until it was too late for them to escape the harm of Hitler. All across Europe people would starve and seek shelter in the hills of their countries; many would be forced to try and eat grass to survive; and millions would never escape.

At this time the people of Great Britain did not yet know that they would have to send many women and children into the countryside or seashore for safety. They did not know that London would be blitzed, and many people would spend nights of terror hiding underground only to emerge and see what destruction had been caused by the bombings. Not only would homes be missing, but great craters would be left throughout Europe's cities, and food would be rationed everywhere.

But as they arrived, Rositha and Vilma felt like the only new people in London. At the suggestion of Julijana they had written ahead and had the address of a ladies' boarding house which promised to have a double room held for them. They even had a small hand-drawn map the landlady had been kind enough to sketch for them, but they could not fathom where to begin. Having the terminal behind them helped to eliminate many possible directions. They would just have to move forward, get across the great open area, and journey up one of several side streets which met the terminal area like the spokes of a wheel. Surely they could change direction via a cross street if that became necessary, but they must move forward.

Being careful not to be trampled, they dashed across the cobblestones to the sidewalk up ahead. Here there were huge warehouses, stores, and more traffic to dodge until they were able to round a corner and find themselves on a side street. Their savings would not last long, so they must immediately look for work once settled into their room. Rositha suggested that as they followed their little map they must also take note of any business which might possibly offer them employment.

Approximately one block up from the terminal, Rositha ventured into a saddler shop where a man was wearing a leather apron and braiding what appeared to be leather straps. She politely asked using her best English, if he could point them towards Big Ben, for that was a reference point for the neighborhood of their lodging. He gave the girls a strange glance and then pointed to the right of the street which they were on. Emboldened by her success in receiving an answer, she then asked, "And if you are needing any assistance with your vork my sister and I are both looking for employment. Ve are experienced seamstresses" she hastened to add judging that would be of help for his business.

Now he formed a sneer on his face. He dropped his work and rose to his full height stepping away from the counter he had been leaning on. Rather loudly he said, "And it will be a bloody cold day in hell before I hire any frauleins in this shop! Get on with ya."

The girls did not understand what had just happened, but the fellow seemed to be angry with them. It seemed best to get about the task of finding their quarters and regrouping after that. They walked hastily out of the shop turning in the direction he had indicated.

15

THE ACCENT LONDON FOUND IN QUESTION

The two Slovenian women eventually found their way through enough of the city to locate the Boarding House for Christian Women, as it was called. They were pleased to be in a home where they could anticipate "kindness to the stranger" as the bible promoted through many parables. But they soon became aware that a Christian home could have some inhabitants not in a state of grace. There were girls there who seemed highly competitive when it came to sharing information on how one might find work. They didn't want to share information which might mean others could have the same things they had, or might possibly become competition at work, or even more importantly, competition for men.

It seemed that the number one goal of the girls in this house was to find a man and marry before he could possibly go off to war or leave the area. These were the girls who were constantly complaining of the shortage of silk stockings, or the price of a frock, as they struggled to remain attractive and, naturally, to be more attractive than any of the other single women within their neighborhoods. There was a bulletin board posted in the front hall of the home which described various dances and socials where the party givers were soliciting young women to attend so that service men might be entertained. Rositha asked what this meant and was informed if she had a party dress she should come along with a group from this house. She simply had to be willing to dance with the men who would be there.

This seemed a little suspect to Rositha and Vilma who had always had a brother take them to even church-sponsored dances, but they rationalized that times were changing with a war coming, and more young people would be far from home. Vilma said, "Let's go, Rositha. Why did we travel so far from home if all we planned to do was sit in the parlor and play cards?"

So, somewhat reluctantly, both girls began to participate in these dance activities, although neither of them would leave a dance with a gentleman she had just met. However, over time they continued to see some of the same men, and thus friendships were developed. Rositha and Vilma even began to go to a few pubs after the dances closed down and were learning to drink beer. It wasn't too long before these pretty young women from Slovenia had to end some evenings abruptly with gentlemen who proved to be too aggressive. At least Rositha thought that they were leaving the men soon enough, but she was always the first one home, so she wasn't absolutely certain of her sister's choices. She was concerned enough to remind Vilma of the risks of going too far with a man, to which Vilma only laughed and said, "Yah, yah, yah."

The dance halls were not fancy. Most were in the basements of churches, in town buildings, or even school gymnasiums. This space had been provided for the various military groups so that the men would keep their spirits up, and the drinks and food were cheap.

Typically, there was no charge for the young women to attend as their presence was a key factor in entertaining the men. These socials were also called "mixers" and gave men who had a night free, someplace to go to relax and meet single girls. The "after hours pubs" could also be simple beer houses, although a few were known to have backrooms for gambling, or for a few minutes of privacy with a girl. Certainly this later type was not the place for good Catholic girls.

However, the only way Rositha and Vilma could afford to attend the socials was if there was free food and drink. After a few weeks, they were saving every penny for their room fees as they had still not found work. It seemed every employer they approached took an instant dislike to them the minute they spoke. Finally, they started applying separately for any job that either of them heard about, hoping that one at a time; they could overcome the fear which their accents generated. Rositha now even started her interviews off with the sentence "I know you may think that my accent is German, and my home language is similar to German, but I have no affiliation with Germany or the Third Reich. My family is Slovenian and I have come here with one sister in an attempt to leave the Axis sentiments behind. I much prefer democracy and the walues of the United Kingdom."

This did not instantly evoke enough sympathy to bring a job within Rositha's reach, but a neighbor of their landlady accepted a reference from her vouching for the character of Vilma. Vilma began a full-time job, six days a week, assisting the nanny of a wealthy family who was within bicycling distance of their boarding house. Vilma was pleased and enjoyed the children. She also was willing to purchase any essentials which Rositha might need. Thus, they were both able to last a bit longer in their original arrangement. Thankfully, it wasn't too much longer before a very prominent British family was willing to hire Rositha. They required additional service, as the master had just been given peerage by Winston Churchill and would sit for Labor in the House of Lords. Their mansion in Barlaston, in the County of Staffordshire, was too far from Parliament, so they were also seeking a home in London. Therefore, Lord and Lady Wedgwood were willing to hire a Slovenian woman. The family business of fine pottery would of course, remain where it had been for several generations, in Staffordshire.

This began a chapter in Rositha's life where she had to wear a pressed uniform with cap and apron every day; speak only when spoken to; learn how to set a proper formal table, and to serve high tea. She was glad for this work because it put food on their table and allowed her to not feel too obliged to the men who would want to ask her to dance. The Wedgwoods also were kindly disposed toward her, understanding that she was a refugee who just happened to have a Germanic accent. That she, herself, was not a political or evil force. There were times when they would send some delectable leftovers home with her and she and Vilma would enjoy a feast.

Soon the war began in earnest with additional hardship every-where, even though the girls were now well fed. Many of her nights back in the boarding house were interrupted by the wailing of sirens. She and Vilma would run with the other women to the underground and hide for hours until an "all clear signal" was sounded. But, while they were in hiding, there would be times when the people around them would become hysterical, screaming and crying and swearing that they were all about to die! Babies would shriek, but sometimes the babies' parents would scream as well. Anxious people became more so, and people with feelings of guilt would imagine that God was punishing them for their crimes; they would say so, and then be certain their death was imminent. When the danger ended for that night, many would not be able to let the fear go and would fear leaving the shelters. Day after day it was a horrible mess with each episode weakening those who were already fragile.

That is not to deny that brave people were emerging. In some sense they were all brave people to survive and return to continue the effort to survive yet again. But some were always reassuring the others, telling stories which took their minds off the current situation, and painting a landscape of beauty where the others could allow their minds to escape. One of these women was Rositha. She even asked if anyone minded if she prayed for them all, and there was no one who declined in this "fox hole." Rositha's rosary was able to provide strength to all who lay in hiding with her even though there were few Catholics among them.

One woman asked if Rositha always came to this underground when the sirens sounded. She then made it her goal to seek Rositha out whenever she could. She needed the strength she felt from this Slovenian woman with her optimism. As time went by, they became friends until one night, now into 1943; she asked Rositha if she would like a blind date.

"I suppose I would if he is a nice man," Rositha said, "But I have not had much luck with dating."

"Well," said her friend, "He is an American, a GI, and my boy-friend says that he would like to meet a nice woman. You know my Fred is an American? They are so generous and have so much more money than the British soldiers; it is fun to be with them."

Rositha shrugged, "If you say so," she said. "But it has been my experience that the more they spend the more they want."

And her friend replied, "You have to loosen up a little if you want to have fun. You know these GIs are here to help our country, and they risk their lives to do it. Everyone just wants to have a little fun."

Rositha said, "I suppose there is no harm in meeting him. Tell me what you know about him; how old is he, is he tall?"

And her friend described him, mentioning that he was born in 1914, which made him two years younger than Rositha. That was the night that, forever after, Rositha, born in 1912, would tell everyone that she was born in 1918, and she was attractive enough that she got away with this for many years.

16

UNLEASHING HORROR
ALL OVER THE WORLD

Adolf Hitler physically began the war by invading the countries near Germany which he wished to possess. He would assure many leaders that he wasn't after them, only wanted their cooperation, as he annexed their neighbor, or rid them of their Jews, but it wasn't long before his actions within other countries, or his actions within their own, demonstrated his true intentions. And most countries did not desire the extermination of any one faction of their people. Like a bridegroom who purports to love his wife, but is secretly a sadistic control-obsessed maniac, his whips and chains would begin to lash and clank in the night; then in broad daylight.

Hitler had always believed that Austria should belong to Germany. She bordered Germany, her people were German speaking, and it was the land of his birth. He also accurately assessed that many Austrians were sympathetic to him, and to the values propagated by the Third Reich. His troops marched into Austria on March 12, 1938, and he fought those who opposed him. But the greatest damage occurred later in the war, in Vienna which was hit by the Allies, chiefly the

United States, and some 57,000 houses would be lost. Austria lacked heavy industry so that only Vienna was a primary focus chiefly due to oil supplies.

But this bombing did not occur until 1943 when the United States planes could reach it from an Italian base. The Fuhrer had left his former Hitler Youth leader, Bauder von Schirach, in charge of Austria. He would send 185,000 Austrian Jews to their deaths in Austrian and Polish concentration camps while von Schirach lived in Hofburg Palace and enjoyed the culture of Vienna.

Prior to the actual aggressions, Hitler had been strategic in his madness; slowly building up believers and inculcating them with his paranoia and hatreds; giving his followers something to hate and a group to blame for their own failings; pressuring manufacturers to produce war supplies instead of peacetime products; rewarding those who followed him and spreading as much propaganda as he could within the youth of the time. Currying favor with other dictators and promising them incredible rewards through the promised growth of their lands should they join with him, was also part of his strategy.

Among his great weaknesses was his greed. He would not listen when his generals, or Axis partners, suggested that he slow down, or not escalate the war too rapidly; that he was fighting on too many fronts, or that he was spread too thin. His troops could be starving, low on fuel, and out of supplies, but he would mount an additional campaign. Instead of regrouping and setting priorities, he not only attacked his neighbors, but took on the Soviet Union later in the war, even though the vastness of this land, and the climate, made it an impossible challenge. A megalomaniac narcissist, he could not accept reports that he was losing ground. He was not capable of accepting reality in time to salvage anything from his obsessive and poisonous plans. And when he knew that the Allies were about to liberate the concentration camps, and set the poor starving prisoners free, his sick mind was desperate for a way to still "win." He accelerated what he had long called the "Final Solution." He did that by ordering the concentration camp guards to exterminate all remaining Jews as fast as they could. That was his solution; fortunately, by this point, the end of the war was so obvious to most that the guards no longer felt compelled to kill the thousands of sick and emaciated prisoners who remained within their camps.

But before we come to the end of the war, we must look a little more deeply at the family we are following to see how they have managed through this long ordeal. Julijana, in Austria, only dared to have but one child because the war was going on all around them. The day Austria was invaded, she reminded Hansi of his claim that they would be safe because he had a special feeling for Hitler and knew that they would be protected. "Now," she said, "where is that protection? Where can we be safe? How can we keep Peter from coming to harm?"

He replied, "This is the time that I will call on my friends and get answers to your questions. Do not panic. We will be okay." But the voice she heard was devoid of his usual confidence. He was prepared to carry Nazi credentials, and meet these men for secret discussions, but he did not know what they would offer him, or what the Nazi friends might expect from him. The heaviest thing, other than Peter, that Hansi had ever carried was his paint brush. Clearly, he would not be "fighting until death for the Fatherland" as they were taught to do in their meetings.

They did not have long to wait to find out what was wanted. They were asked to move to an apartment in the city of Linz on the

Danube. It was a lovely apartment and came with elegant furnishings. It would take months before Julijana would understand their good fortune. Here there were many meetings for Hansi to attend, official portraits for him to paint, and their dwelling was considered safe. His artwork was important to the Fuhrer. Although they would never meet again, he was asked to paint a portrait of Hitler from a photograph.

While Hansi helped with some administrative jobs, in addition to the paintings, Julijana was needed as a factory worker to be sure there were enough munitions sent to the front, along with bandages. She was bored by this work but felt she must prove herself to the superiors or risk some kind of punishment. It seemed that everyone was wary of everyone else; so many people wanted to get ahead that no one was trustworthy. If you provided an opening, someone would be happy to report you for any and all conceivable misdeeds. Julijana always thought about her little son, taken in and cared for by Hansi, and how she owed everything to him. If Hansi needed her to fold bandages for the duration of the war, then she would do that.

Then there were some very pleasant evenings, too. Officers of high rank, who had just had their portraits painted by her husband, would invite them out to dine. They were expected to wear fancy clothing and ate very well. With rationing, they often went most of the week with no meat, but with this group they could enjoy a fish first course, a meat filled entre, and all the alcohol they wished. The German and Austrian desserts were rich and chocolaty and rare treats during the war. Julijana feared she would be the only person she knew gaining, rather than losing weight. She felt a deep pang of guilt not knowing how her siblings were doing, but then chose to block these pangs from her mind so that she could fit in with her husband's crowd.

On the days she did not work she enjoyed walking around in Linz. It was a lovely old city built along the Danube with a long harbor which she found pleasant for walking; and then a wide cobblestone courtyard which seemed the center of town. On one side there was a labyrinth of little streets with shops such as saddlers, chocolate makers, confections, clothing, wine and a butcher shop at the far end. These streets surrounded a large hotel which had a grand restaurant on the ground floor. This was a favorite meeting place of the Nazi organization to which Hanzi belonged. When the weather permitted, they always took their meals into the courtyard where the restaurant placed tables on the cobblestones. Here they could enjoy the ambiance of a large fountain and the occasional street musician.

On the opposite side of the courtyard were multistory apartment houses. Many were stucco and had window boxes overlooking a central courtyard hidden from the more open area. One must own an apartment to gain access to this area. The window boxes and the flowers they contained were all brightly colored. There was a neatness and symmetry to everything in this neighborhood.

This central square had the Danube on one side, the hotel and little shops to the right, the apartments and some smaller restaurants on the left, and then straight back and up an incline was a street along which were churches and a synagogue. Julijana ventured up what she jokingly referred to as "Holy Avenue," so that she could admire the architecture. But she could not understand why the synagogue was boarded up and swastikas were painted on it. Also, the gate was not simply locked but heavily barred as well. She did not understand what had happened but planned to find out.

17

KRISTALLNACHT WAS NOT JUST IN GERMANY

Julijana had time to walk around and explore Linz on her days off. Hansi was busy with his painting and propaganda meetings, and Peter was in school, which left her free to discover shops, neighborhoods, and to meet people. On this particular sunny afternoon, as she was staring at the abandoned and beaten synagogue, a woman was walking toward her. Julijana said, "Pardon me, I am new to Linz. Could you tell me what has happened to this building?" and she pointed to the temple beside her.

"Well," was the reply, "all spring, after the Germans arrived, there was trouble in this city, and all across Austria. There was violence everywhere, and it went from a few incidents to riots, on a nightly basis. This was from March, throughout that Spring, Summer, and until early November. The Jews were not happy with how they were being treated. More and more they were being forced from their homes so the occupation soldiers could have housing."

"By November, Hitler's SS troopers would pull Jews off the streets to try and prevent more riots. Then they were found congregating in the synagogues, maybe having secret meetings, so the troopers had to take control. They went in and broke the windows, and a few rabbis may have been injured. They were all crying and carrying on. After that night, more Jews were sent to the camps, like the one about 16 kilometers from here. Now things are much more peaceful." And, after these remarks, the woman continued on her way, leaving Julijana standing there with her mouth wide open. She was astounded that this had been going on under their very noses, and wondered how she could have been so self-absorbed as to miss it all.

And this woman's remarks left her ice cold. There seemed to be no sympathy connected to her words, certainly no empathy. Of course people were angry and upset if they were forced from their homes. Who would not be? And was this woman suggesting that Jews who decried their losses were at fault? That sending them all to camps for the peace of the neighborhoods was an equitable solution? She spoke as though these families and home owners should intrinsically know they must give up their space for the SS troops? How could this be right?

She had known about some of the violence, for they heard shouting in the streets, but they had been moving last November, and must have been in transit when this destruction occurred. So their German friends were responsible for this turmoil and displacement of people. How horrible, she thought, but then she began to imagine how it had happened, since she had seen many people wearing stars with the word JUDE in the center. She had not previously guessed at why some people were required to wear labels. Then she thought my husband is a German; I will ask him about this tonight.

But that evening they were expected to dine with a large group out on the square in front of the restaurant. It seemed far too public a place, and much too political a group, to ask her question. She would wait until the next morning when Peter left for school. Surely, Hansi would have a reasonable explanation for this bizarre and violent behavior.

And what did that woman mean about a "camp" up the road a few kilometers? What kind of a camp did they send grownups to? Perhaps they could ride by it some weekend. While she thought of these questions, something was troubling her. If people were being labeled, and removed forcibly from their homes and churches, this did not sound like a pleasant situation. What about their apartment with the good light and lovely view; who had vacated it in such a hurry that some clothing and lovely furnishings had been left behind? Could they be occupying the home of Jews who had not chosen to leave but who were now unhappily in a camp somewhere? It had all seemed too good to be true. Hansi would need to tell her everything that was going on. She wasn't raised to take things in this way. Jesus was humble and cared for the least among them. What would her mother think? And then she recalled how the priest had treated her and abandoned her with a few dinars when it suited him. Perhaps the world was not as she had thought it.

Julijana did not sleep well that night. She dreamed of waking up in the night and coming out to the kitchen for a glass of water and perhaps a snack. When she got to the kitchen, a family of three, just like hers with two parents and a young child, were seated at the kitchen table their heads bowed. Each person was praying for more food as their dishes were empty. They could not see Julijana, but they spoke of having everything taken from them. The woman cried that she would never see her mother's diamonds again. The man held her hand and said, "But we have each other."

To which the boy responded, "But Papa, I have heard that we will be taken away and must all work for the Nazis." Then they all began to sob, and Julijana did not know how to respond, or if she could even speak to them. The room became very hot, and she saw the kitchen table starting to melt onto the floor as though it were made of wax. Soon the family members' feet were covered in hot wax, and they were writhing in pain. She went to get a pan of water from the sink to bring to them, but her feet were glued to the floor. She could neither retreat, nor move forward just watch the horror of the family trapped in this kitchen and melting into the floor. Finally, she returned to her bedroom, where she also imagined that she was in bed with her husband and three total strangers.

Foggy eyed at breakfast, Julijana was nevertheless anxious to ask Hansi, "What is this camp I have heard about located just outside of town? Why are the Germans living in the homes of Jews; and what is the purpose of these camps? I don't know how you can keep people from their own homes for a very long time?"

Hansi replied that, "You must simply calm down, my dear. Look at what we have now that we did not have a few years ago? Not only do we have a strong son who is going to an excellent school, but we have a beautiful apartment, all the food we could possibly consume, and many fine friends who always wish to be with us. Everything is wunderbar! We should be happy - you should be happy!"

"But you must be careful of the questions you ask and of whom you ask them. Do not trust the stranger on the street to be a kind person. They might be someone who would like to report you! Maybe they would like to move into this apartment and enjoy this view. Do not let them know you question anyone, nor listen should they criticize the Fuhrer. Even in front of our friends, there might be jealousies, and you want to be careful that they do not push us out of this home we now have. Speak only to me of these matters, and do so quietly, please."

"Well then, one more question of you my husband," Julijana added. "Where did the Jews go who used to own this apartment, and these fine furnishings? Where are they now and how do they live?"

"Ach," Hansi replied, now seeming vexed. "You asked about the camps, the camps are for them. They stay in these camps to become vigorous with the fine country air, and then they are moved to several major relocation areas in Poland where they can be with more of their own kind and establish new synagogues there together as a group. Less trouble for respectable Germans and more support of their own people. Now please, let us not argue over this!"

This information, and the way it was delivered, rocked Julijana to her marrow. She had been raised as a peasant on a struggling farm and had only the beauty of nature, and her family to carry as pride. She had arrived in Austria in dire straits, for she was with child, had very little money, and no sure plan to support herself. Everything she had she felt she owed to Hansi, who had always seemed a good and hardworking man. But now, the love of her life wanted her to accept that they were entitled to those things for which another family had worked and sacrificed, simply because he worked for the Germans. This did not make sense.

Julijana was deeply depressed for the next few days and struggling to keep her family and their friends from noticing this mental state, when a telegram finally made its way to their door. This message from her father contained the news that her mother had passed away, been taken by the angels to heaven, and her dying words sent love to all her family.

Then Julijana could openly weep and show her deep pain without question. But while she was suffering with this loss, she continued to think of those other families in great pain. She vowed on her mother's grave that she would find out just what these camps were all about; she would endeavor to see one.

18

SEEKING ANSWERS FOR QUESTIONS
SHE COULD NOT ASK

Julijana awoke in the middle of the night and silently made her way to the kitchen. She wanted to see if the little family was there again, at her table, or more correctly, at their table. But the kitchen was devoid of anyone, save Julijana. Yet, as she sat where they had been, she could sense their presence. She then made a small mug of chamomile tea hoping it would soothe her enough so that she could go back to sleep. As she blew on the tea to cool it down before drinking, a strong urge came over her. She found a pen and paper and left a note. Without thinking that these people would need to read German, she wrote out "lep pozdrav," kind regards, in Slovenian. She wanted them to know that she thought of them as friends.

By morning, Julijana realized that Hansi would not help her solve the mystery of why these people had left their home and why their synagogue had been so badly vandalized. She waited for him to go to the studio to work and for Peter to be at school. Then, taking most of her grocery money, she made her way the short distance to the train depot. It was removed a bit from the town to help keep the city clean but was not far from the Danube, so that shipping could be connected between water and rail. Before the war was over, this area would be bombed to prevent supplies from getting through to the Axis, but at the moment, it was still much in use.

Fearing that she might be the object of scrutiny on this quest, Julijana had intentionally dressed in quite respectable clothing. She wore a jacket with wide shoulders, for such was the fashion at this time, and a small amount of fur on the lapels. The fur indicated a person of some means as this style was associated with the upper classes. She had found the coat in a closet within the back of the house and thought this would be an ideal time to put it to use.

She approached the station's ticket sales window and asked for a round trip ticket, same day, to Mauthausen. "Mauthausen?" said the attendant. His voice was raised, as well as his bushy eyebrows, and he seemed genuinely shocked. "Frau, what business could a lady like you have at Mauthausen?"

She paled and stammered a bit, not having anticipated being asked to explain herself. "I have business there, not that it should concern you." And she stood as tall as she could manage.

"And do you know what you will find out there?"

"Yes," she replied, "A camp where many people await transportation to Poland for reunification with their families."

This struck the railroad worker as amazingly funny, for he tipped his head back and roared with laughter until he could not catch his breath, sounding more like one of his train engines trying to build up steam, than a man. "I think you had better get permission from the commandant before you head in that direction and, for that matter, from your husband, too. It is no place for a lady unless you are an officer, which I very much doubt," he said.

Not knowing when to let go of the argument, Julijana retorted, "And what harm is there if I only wish to see the Camp and take the return train home?"

The ticket seller then added, "So you know about the camp? And who has been telling you such stories, my dear Frau? I must insist on seeing your papers. I am not entirely certain that your intentions are in keeping with the values of the Reich." And he put his hand out to her as though to immediately receive the papers.

She began walking backwards. "I only meant to purchase a ticket today, not to take the journey. I will return with my papers tomorrow." And she hastily walked away, forcing herself not to reveal her panic by breaking into a run.

By the time she returned home, Julijana was convinced that this had been a foolish mission for her, and that she would be better off if Hansi were not made aware of the incident. She hastily changed into her usual housedress and secreted the lovely coat back into the recesses of the storage closet. There, she thought, that is over with, but she was not so fortunate.

Linz is a city, but it is made up of a series of small neighborhoods within the city. When she marched out in her fine coat, Julijana might as well have posted a sign asking her neighbors to join her for a train trip, for a series of eyes and tongues had followed her. While Julijana was helping Peter with his studies, and drawing his bath that evening, for this apartment had a lovely en suite full bathroom, Hansi went out for a stein of beer with his friends. It seemed only fair, he said, as he had been cooped up in his studio all day.

When he returned, long after the boy had crawled into bed, his entire personality had changed. It wasn't so much that he had over-indulged in alcohol, but that he was angrier than she had ever seen him. Upon his return, he made a great show of banging the door open such that Julijana quickly admonished him to be considerate of the sleeping boy. Then he stood before her, jacket still on, arms extended on either side of his body, clenching and unclenching his fists. His jaw looked hard and tight. When he spoke, his teeth did not seem to move with his mouth, but a fine spray of spittle flew from his lips.

"What did you mean to do when you sought a train ticket this morning?" he asked.

She began, "I don't know what you are talking about? This morning I went out and bought cabbage and peppers at the open market, and then spent the rest of the day making a fine soup for you which we have just eaten. I had no time to go sightseeing."

"Ah," he said, "You may want me to believe this, but you were seen by several people who have met you with me, and they said you were very well dressed for a morning walk, so they kept an eye on you since they were out strolling anyway. You appeared to argue with the man in the train ticket booth, and then march away very rapidly. Now don't lie to me, this could be very serious for all of us!"

Julijana knew she had better tell the truth. Hansi was a good man, but in order to be sure of what was going on, he would not be above taking her to meet the man and demanding an explanation from them both. To be right, and not deceived, he would not mind humiliating her.

She stammered, "I made a terrible mistake and hoped that you would never have to learn of it, as I am very sorry and so embarrassed. I wanted to see the camp where the former residents of this house are living. I wanted to thank them for the many beautiful things that they left us and see if there was anything which we could do for them. Perhaps they even need the warm coat which I was wearing this morning."

Hansi exploded, "How could you be so stupid, Julijana? I always thought that you were a bright woman, kind-hearted, but not a fool. Do you know what one of our Fuhrer's primary goals is? He wants to eradicate Jews from the face of the earth! He doesn't believe these people are fit to live around us! He has been moving them to camps where they will either work for him or die! Do you think he wants you to go bring jackets and coats to them? Does he want you to worry about them and pray over them? NO! NO! NO! And you will stop this kind of behavior immediately or I shall have to lock you in the house!"

"The Gestapo would be happy to include you in the camps and let you share their fate if you are so inclined. And they will take me and Peter too just to wipe out any trouble we might be inclined to cause. This is not a game! This is dead serious. We will lose our home and our jobs if you don't mind your own business!" Then he grabbed her by the shoulders, and for a moment she feared that she would be hit, but he only shook her a little and demanded that she say, "Yes, I understand."

"All right then," he said. "Let us never speak of this again. When the neighbors ask questions we will say it was all a misunderstanding, and change the subject."

"Yes, Hansi," she repeated, and went into the kitchen to lay out the dishes for breakfast.

But her heart was heavy with the weight of knowing her inaction was as venial as a sin of commission. If she did nothing, knowing what must be going on in this nearby camp, where the very owners of her apartment had been taken, then she bore the sin of murder.

And her heart added the words, "forever a mark on her soul." And she could clearly picture this family complete with a young child. They were starving, wearing rags and all close to tears.

She would try living with Hansi's rules but was not certain that she could do so without losing her mind.

19

LIFE: THE FAVOR OF A LIFETIME

The next day, Julijana tried to carry out her general duties as normally as possible. She was self-censoring her movements, as she was certain that Hansi or the "neighborhood spies," would be watching her every move. For example, she would not wear anything that might make her appear to be flaunting her better clothing, or dressing too poorly. She also carried only two shopping bags so that her purchases might not appear to be conspicuous consumption. Still, she had felt relief when he had handed her the normal grocery allowance so that she was free to conduct her usual rounds of the shops. She didn't want to be a prisoner in her own home and enjoyed purchasing the ingredients which would turn into a good meal for them. Cooking was one of the few pleasures she had left while this weight of guilt hung so heavily upon her that, at times, she could barely lift her eyes.

She went out into the square where each morning an open market was assembled and then taken down by early afternoon. She liked to shop early to get the best fruit and vegetables. After a few hours the choicest selections were picked over and often only damaged fruit and vegetables remained. Having grown up on a farm, she did not care for food that had been handled by many other people. Certainly, she always scrubbed the food before she cooked it but still preferred the unhandled. And, as times were difficult during the war, many things were at a shortage even in this German-dominated city, as the troops must be fed first. So the rule was to go early if you wanted something in particular, or you would need to serve whatever had not been chosen, if anything at all. This would usually mean making a cabbage and carrot soup, with a bit of onion if you were lucky. This was nothing that Hansi would care for, thus his willingness to trust the shopping to Julijana, so that he could paint by the morning light.

As she moved from stall to stall in the open market, Julijana could see that the size of the cubicles was shrinking from week to week both in numbers and in girth. Fewer farmers had less and less to sell. But some of the basics were still there so that she could acquire a half-pound of ground beef, a few ears of dried corn, and two large potatoes. As she turned a bit hurriedly, to approach another bin of food a few yards away, she felt a child clutch at her apron. She looked down to see a shabbily clad lad who seemed to be trying to get her attention rather than attempting to steal anything.

"Please, Frau," he said sounding rather desperate. "I understand that you are interested in the plight of my aunt, uncle and cousin who are residing at the camp by the river?"

She took his hand as though they were friends and smiled at him as she walked away from anyone within earshot. "What may I do for you young man?" she said rather formally.

"I understand you are living in their apartment and were thinking of visiting them?" he said.

She quickly silenced him with a stern gaze. She lowered her voice and almost squeezed his hand in half as she demanded to know what she could do for him. He stammered, "They are in grave danger and will soon be transported to a death camp or moved toward a place of death where they now live. I live in the woods and try to go between them and home. Please, if we had a small boat and someone to move them by the end of next week, it would save their lives."

She could hear the pleading in his voice, and she saw his eyes well up with tears. This was no childhood attempt at pilfering a few coins from her food budget; this was a desperate child trying to aid his family in a fight for their lives.

"How did you happen to come to me?" she asked.

"I told you," he said. "Someone has been watching their apartment to see what happens to their things, and you were observed talking to the ticket man at the railroad. They said you seemed like a good woman and not a murderer. We are without money and must beg for any assistance possible, but they are surrounded by water on an island at this camp. I can lead them to others in the woods, but first they must get to me. I have a plan, but no boat, and am not, as you can see, big enough to row one should I come by such a thing."

"Yes," said Julijana. "I can see you need someone to row for you. Meet me back here in three days, at the side of the egg seller's stand, and I will tell you if there is help. And say nothing to anyone about this. Do you understand?" And nodding his head in agreement, he disappeared from the market.

Julijana was not sure if she even slept a wink that night. She continuously mulled over the "whos and hows" of this situation, and she kept coming back to the same solution. She would have to be in touch with Mojca and Vid. They were among the few people she could trust not to turn her in to the Nazis and they both had the skills and strength to manage a boat. While Julijana had once been a strong rower, she had not even been in a boat since first leaving Slovenia while pregnant with Peter. If this "mission" as she now thought of it, required any strenuous work, her arms could not be trusted to fulfill the duties. And, as she could also not imagine having an opportunity to disappear long enough from Hansi's side to conduct such a project, she knew help was needed.

Her first dilemma was how to find Mojca and Vid, if they were actually still in Austria. The last time they had spoken she had thought their trip to Australia might be happening soon. She had better call as soon as she could and pray it was not too late. Her only backup plan was to go herself to perform this rescue and she was most uncertain of the likelihood that she would be successful. She hurried to the hallway where they had a phone, and was grateful that Hansi was not now at home. There was no answer at the old apartment number which was all she had for a contact. This date was prior to the bombings of Vienna by the Americans so there was still hope that the lines were not down, but the war had evoked a great deal of difficulty in all communications.

She nervously organized the kitchen and performed her housework in record time. She wanted to place the call again before Hansi could come home for lunch but did not wish to call too soon. Finally, she could contain herself no longer and rushed back to the phone. Her nerves caused her to misspeak to the operator, and she twice had to repeat the phone number before the connection could be made. Then she heard ringing on the other end. After five rings, she started to perspire profusely, after eight; she began to fear she must again ring off. Then two things happened simultaneously: Mojca answered the phone, and Hansi walked into the apartment.

Julijana had to pretend that she was both happy to see Hansi and not overjoyed, though she was, to hear Mojca's voice. She gave Hansi a bright smile and a wave before focusing completely on her sister to whom she must communicate an urgent and dangerous request, without using the words which would cause Hansi to intervene.

"I am so pleased to hear your voice, Mojca," she said. "Hansi has just arrived home for lunch, but I must take advantage of this opportunity to speak with you, for I fear you will soon be too far away for calls. Are you still planning to go to Australia for the rest of your life?" She tried to sound amused, although this thought broke her heart.

She listened, and then spoke again. "That soon?" she said. "Well, I don't blame you. Every country in Europe is in trouble, it seems. Is there any chance that you and Vid could visit us here for one last time before you go? We really have plenty of room, and food isn't much of a problem unless Vid requires steak?" Pause and listening then:

"Are you sure? It would mean so much to me, to Peter and Hansi too. We really don't have much family these days."

Then an explosive; "Danke, Danke, we will see you Saturday!"

And with that, Julijana turned to her husband chattering excitedly about her sister's and Vid's almost-surprise visit to bid them auf Wiedersehen before leaving for Australia.

20

A MOST CLEVER BOY
LEADS THE WAY

On Thursday, three days from their first meeting, and just two before Mojca and Vid were expected to arrive for their visit, Julijana sought out the young boy at the egg vendor's booth in the market. He must have been lurking near-by watching for her, because as soon as she came near this kiosk, he was beside her. They pretended to look for cracked eggs and selected a few whole ones for her basket, then she paid the dealer and they walked around the side of the large stone building and into its shadows.

"I don't even know your name," said Julijana.

"It's Abraham," said the child.

"All right, Abraham, you have two excellent rowers. I think that they will agree to help you, but you must be certain, absolutely certain, of their safety. It is a couple, and she is my sister. My very precious sister, do you understand?"

"I do," he said. "And when will we go? I must have a wagon ready to get them close to the camp near the river."

"Please," said Julijana, "give me two nights with them and then you may have them on Monday. Is Monday all right?"

"Yes," said the boy, his dark brows furrowed, "I will make it all right. And tell me; how they will react if I am stealing a boat in front them?"

"I suppose they will accept this as necessary, but please no violence."

"Okay," said the boy, and hoped this was true, but he had his fingers crossed behind his back just in case there were to be a problem. Then he arranged to meet them behind a nearby tree that they could see from their spot in the market at 2:30 Monday afternoon. He would take care of all the rest.

Half shaking, and half laughing, Julijana left quickly with her makings for an omelet held close to her body. She would garner other ingredients tomorrow to prepare for her darling guests whom she was about to send into danger; danger so unthinkable that she did not even herself comprehend it. She felt it urgent now to make everything lovely at home. She did not want Hansi to suspect that anything unusual was going on behind the scenes of their life as a happy and loyal German couple.

The remainder of the day passed in a cheerful appearing but mild panic for Julijana, who kept thinking of all that could possibly go wrong, not the least of which was the fact that she had not yet even asked Mojca and Vid to take on this mission. To help quiet her nerves, Julijana peeled some apples to make a pie, and sliced cabbage to let it season a little with vinegar, caraway seeds and a few more apples. She reasoned that if the food was good they might be more inclined to say yes to her dangerous request. They also had likely not eaten well over the last few months, when all rations were first determined necessary for the troops and then what remained were sent along for civilian needs. There were many complaints, but the same method was used for the distribution of warm clothing and boots. She and Hansi would appear to have an opulent lifestyle to her sister and Vid.

The next day Julijana completed her purchases for the meals she was planning for her guests and family. She thought how light-hearted she might ordinarily be if her guests were not about to embark on a dangerous sojourn which she was requesting. Then she thought again of just how awful this entire situation was and that she should never be light-hearted again until this terrible war was over: she day-dreamed for a moment of how her childhood worries had been simple, and the solutions within her grasp, but how fortunate she was to have Peter for a son.

Then she blinked away a few tears recalling her mother's support and became more determined to accomplish this goal of extending help to others who were trapped by Hitler's madness. Somehow they would pull off this escape. Hansi might never know of what she was capable, but she would know and believe in herself.

Vid and Mojca arrived with stories of slow trains and stop points where they had to keep showing their identification and stating the reason for which they were traveling. No one, however, tried to refuse them continued progress, as they appeared to be two young lovers on a family mission before he was to join the Nazis forces as a foreign sympathizer. That was the story they had practiced, and it seemed to hold up.

Once in Julijana's kitchen, with its hanging sausages, fermenting coleslaw, and cooling apple pie, they were so seduced by the abundance and her generosity, that their worry and inconvenience was a minor matter. They even enjoyed a cup of real coffee before Julijana convinced them to have some sweet German white wine before lunch. Soon it was an occasion of considerable merriment. Then, a short time before Hansi was to join them, and while Peter was still at his Hitler Youth Meeting; Julijana told them the whole story.

She explained how Hansi had attained this house, to whom it really belonged, and why she felt so concerned for this family. When Mojca and Vid were most sympathetic to this family, she went further, explaining that she knew where they were being held, and she knew that they were in imminent danger. Again, her sister and Vid were most concerned and even asked "Can we be of help?"

With this, perhaps perfunctory comment, she could hold back her request for assistance no longer, and she explained about Abraham and his need for rowers. Then she gave them every possible reason why they should say no to this request. She also described multiple dangers she could imagine, exaggerating every possibility for them to see. Then she explained how she could not even get away from Hansi long enough for an afternoon train trip to the site that she was, in fact, requesting that they go with the boy.

Mojca was the first to speak. "I have spent most of my life living on Lake Bled and have had a wonderful life. I love boats and the water, but most of all I love rowing and the smooth pull on muscles and arms. This mission was made for me. When do we go?"

Cringing with both shame and embarrassed joy, Julijana said, "We must now stop talking about this as Hansi and Peter will soon be home, but I will take you to meet Abraham on Monday afternoon. He will have a wagon for the trip and more details. He knows the woods and the river and will be your guide."

With that assurance they went back to their festive mood so that Hansi and Peter should not become aware of the situation which would soon unfold. Vid was a bit concerned, for he feared anything that might threaten Mojca, but she was delighted, as it had been several years since she had felt her strength was of importance to anyone, and she had wished for an opportunity to fight against the Nazis.

21

ROW, ROW, ROW YOUR BOAT AND NOBODY SCREAM

Monday afternoon came too fast for Julijana. She knew she might never see her sister and Vid again. She also feared that the reason for this might not simply be their choice of moving to Australia, but the danger she had placed them in while attempting to save an unknown family. Her hands shook all morning as she prepared their breakfast and a meal for their "train trip" back. She had to be so careful to hide this trembling from Hansi and Peter; all that saved her was Peter going to school early and Hansi going down to the studio for an appointment. She managed to hold herself together until they had left the apartment.

Now she was getting through this frightening time by putting one foot in front of the other. She just continued to urge herself to go through the motions of what these next steps required. The day was bright and clear with a little crispness in the air. The Danube modified the coolness with its moisture, even though they were going away from the river initially and connecting with it closer to its source, through the woods. She found herself hoping that Abraham would not show up, and they would simply tell Hansi the visit was to last a little longer. That would keep Vid and Mojca close to her, although it would leave the family in the camp doomed. She could barely handle this situation, in either case, as she was so afraid of what might befall her dear sister.

Then, like the mental anguish of a pending, but badly needed high-risk surgery, the dreaded, yet hoped for moment was upon them, and she must let go of her sister's hand. Their parting was meant to be swift so that fewer townspeople would notice Julijana's involvement with these "strangers," but the hug between the two women lingered. "Don't worry," whispered Mojca, "we are most excited to make this contribution." Then she uttered a statement forbidden for a good Catholic girl to say, followed by the name "Adolf Hitler."

This parting left Julijana both laughing and crying, as she tried to inconspicuously walk back toward her apartment. Even Abraham tried to say a grateful farewell to her, but she was off before she could change her mind and cancel the expedition. Her apartment would seem most quiet tonight without her precious sister there. Still, she would do her best to concentrate on making a tasty meal from their leftovers. Hansi should never become suspicious of her actions or her loyalty.

And toward the woods, the little caravan began its journey. One older wooden wagon with wobbling, rusty, metal rimmed wheels, a handsome young couple with light blond hair, and a slightly swarthy young man who was poorly dressed, did not call a great deal of attention to it. The cover story which they planned to use, that they were on their honeymoon despite the war, for she was with child and they were doing the right thing before he joined Hitler's forces, seemed plausible enough. The boy was unknown to them until a day ago when a cousin had presented the boy's services as a wedding gift so that they might see more of the Danube.

They would, naturally, express great shock that they could possibly be heading into dangerous areas as all they wished to do was see a few wildflowers and perhaps take a boat ride. They would insist that they would not tarry long or associate with anyone along the way. And so their adventure continued not far from the railroad tracks leading to the death camp on the outskirts of an area just outside of Linz; the camp to which Julijana's excursion had been denied, as she was not cleared to visit this place. All around them it seemed like simple woods with a river running close-by, but they often felt as though they were being watched.

After a few hours in which nothing of consequence had happened, and they were admittedly less on guard lulled by these calm surroundings, they turned a corner and were surprised to find several Nazi officers in the pathway. They were ordered to halt and present their papers.

Vid replied to the soldiers, remaining as poised as he had been when they were rehearsing their lines. He presented his wife, as well as explained who their young servant was. He concluded by stating this was but a day trip, at the end of which they must return to Vienna where he would join the forces. It sounded plausible enough, given that he was not a German or Viennese native which would have meant he would long ago have been enlisted. After a few anguished minutes they were permitted to continue along their route but warned not to speak with anyone, and certainly not to offer a ride through these woods to any strangers. When they were well out of earshot Vid remarked, "Good thing we are looking for a boat!"

"And what about the boat," Vid now asked, addressing his comments to Abraham? "When and where will we take to the river?"

Abraham appeared confident with a straight gaze into his questioner's eyes. "There is a small village within a few minutes of here. It is within sight of the river at a scenic spot. Over the years, many families have come to this area for picnics and to gather sweet smelling greens and pinecones to take home. It became so popular that several of the families have built cabins here so that they might sleep by the river. Then these families would bring boats and tables to practically live outside.

"My father says, 'as always happens, once people own a spot where they used to visit, the spot is no longer so intriguing.' So, within a few years of the cabins being built, they were no longer used very frequently. Now, with the war on, some of them appear totally abandoned. That means there are boats abandoned as well. You shall have your pick of many boats, I am certain!"

They moved more rapidly following those remarks, as they were all anxious to shift to the river and take care of this mission. Just as Abraham had predicted, there was a small enclave of cabins within a few minutes of their discussion. The cottages were in a cluster, built all of wood, with designs cut into their shutters, and each with a stone chimney. But none of them looked freshly painted or inhabited; in fact, they gave the appearance of being likely to leak and to, perhaps, contain woodland creatures for residents.

"If the boats are this run-down," said Vid, "I wonder if they will float." And they all looked at each other with eyebrows raised, but not a word was uttered.

Finally, Mojca said, "Let's have a look and hope for the best."

It had been apparent, from their first view of the area, that the cabins were small; perhaps one or two bedrooms with the children likely to be sleeping in a group on mats in the main room. And if the cabins were small, the boats were correspondingly petite. You could not imagine a group going out sightseeing in these, they were not pletna. The husband, and a son or two, might take one out to fish, but if others were interested in fishing, they must be taking turns. And the wooden hull of each of the first two boats they found was filled with water. This water should have been drained out of the boats, or, more correctly the boats should have been propped up on stones, upside down so that no water would have collected in them. Whoever was responsible for these boats had treated them casually, and the result was rot; rot that would render the first two unworthy of holding anything out of the water, for they would never again float.

Finally, the third boat was up on blocks, turned over so it did not collect water, and was even covered over with a tarp. But when Mojca and Vid flipped the boat to its right side, they found a large snake was living underneath it. Mojca had never cared for snakes, and especially when she had not anticipated seeing any, she could barely control herself from screaming and dropping her end of the boat. Fortunately, Abraham was near, and saw that it was harmless and hastened its exit from the area. Then they made certain that this boat was as sturdy as it looked by attempting to poke a few holes in it. It withstood the prodding. However, the maximum number of people it could transport was four, and they had planned that both Vid and Mojca would row the family out. Now they had another dilemma: who would row?

22

DIVIDE AND CONCUR
OR AT LEAST BE SAFE

As they moved the selected boat closer to the spot along the river which was near enough to the camp to gain them access, but not place them in sight of the guards, they continued to discuss how they would transport more than four passengers. The answer was that they could not; therefore, arrangements had to be altered. Finally, it was determined that the three of them, Mojca, Vid and Abraham, would go to the meeting point, but when the family of three joined them, they would be rowed away by Mojca. She was the logical choice as she weighed the least but was a strong oarsman.

Abraham and Vid were thankful that it was July, as they would swim along the side of the boat which was the furthest away from the guards and out of sight. On the return trip, Mojca would get them all to the wagon, and, if the men got tired of swimming along the way, they could hang, for a time, alongside the boat. This was the plan if all went well; there was no plan "B," it seemed this must work, or it wouldn't.

CYNTHIA HERBERT-BRUSCHI ADAMS

They unloaded the boat in the area of the launch and then took the wagon back a few feet tethering the old horse and the wagon out of sight in some bushes. Abraham then announced that perhaps he should explain more: "Mauthausen is not really a camp at all but, by now, a huge fortress all of stone and really impenetrable. My Aunt and Uncle and their small son are actually servants for the guards' quarters and temporarily housed on this bit of island. Mauthausen itself is in the heart of a granite quarry a little further along. I wanted them to be rescued quickly, before their status could change.

"Each prisoner is expected to work at different levels of duty until they are penalized. Then all penalized prisoners, male or female, are forced to carry granite rocks beyond what is humanly possible. And being penalized is not based upon merit, but whether or not the quarry requires more help. The prisoners suffer and live in constant pain. If they collapse from exhaustion, they are killed. However, as soon as the pain is too great, hundreds of these poor people take their own lives by jumping off the cliffs at the quarry's high points. Then the cruel guards mockingly refer to this as 'taking the parachute.'"

This bit of information horrified the unknowing Vid and Morja and all three hastily made the short walk back to what they had jokingly referred to as their "yacht." But this description of Mauthausen had left them no longer in a joking frame of mind. Then, under Abraham's directions, they headed along the river to the rendezvous point with his family.

Their first problem arose because the family was too frightened to look out of their hiding spot until Abraham had to beckon the father by name. After a few sotto vocce cries for "Uncle Saul," the family emerged from behind a rock and an old stump where they had remained covered with moss and dirt for quite some time. They

128

had reasoned that if the guards found them missing and brought out the dogs to find them by scent, the smell of the earth would have distracted the animals from their human odor. They dusted off and hurriedly made their way to the boat crawling in as directed and covering themselves with an old tarp. It was not a time to worry about spiders because the snake likely had taken care of them already.

Once Vid was no longer in the boat, Mojca did not want to admit it, but the rowing was rougher than she had anticipated. His weight was nothing compared with his rowing power. Still, she could have done at least this much a few years back, but city life had taken a toll on her arm strength. She managed to do what was expected. However, her muscles were already aching and her hands raw with blisters. Even the gloves Julijana had insisted that she wear, now had holes in them; it was a rough, heavy, wooden boat, and the oars, unfortunately, matched it.

As they sculled along the far edge of the river trying to remain below the guards' sight line, they hit earth where the water was low; and they hit it hard enough to become embedded in its mud. Initially, Vid and Abraham attempted to pull them free but with no luck. It would have been comical if the consequences of making noise and being spotted had not been so dire. Finally, the family disembarked by standing up to their ankles in mud, while Vid and Mojca pushed and pulled the boat out of the earth. Once they were safely around this little ground swell, the family returned to the boat and the journey continued.

It wasn't long before they were again startled, this time by a campfire surrounded by Nazi Guards. Apparently, being this far removed from the main compound, the night guards were able to stay awake by assembling in one spot and passing a bottle. Any superiors would have seen that they were punished for this lax behavior, but they were currently accountable only to themselves. This was good fortune for the escapees, provided none of them looked into the dark side of the river. If one guard were to spot them, then all guards would have given chase, or taken shots. They could imagine what the punishment was and knew that an escape was not treated casually.

The distance back to the boat landing seemed farther than the distance to the rendezvous, but that was probably due to the extra physical exertion and the time lost in the mud. Now the landing was just discernible by the light of the fully risen moon, and this part of their voyage was complete. They all struggled out of the water, and the women and child went to the wagon to dry off. They were then left with a few towels and a little food while the men and Abraham carried the boat to a secluded area next to the nearest cabin, making it look as though it had been resting in the leaves for months. There was no need to leave evidence for anyone regarding their excursion.

Eventually, the escapees were fed and settled down into the wagon while Vid drove the horse in the direction Abraham indicated. Mojca tried to sleep for a while, but, before she could fully rest, it was time to turn the wagon back in to its owner near Linz. Then they all had to walk.

Once out in the woods, and apparently free, the family began to speak about their ordeal. They had been pulled from their home, their very beds, and on the same night that the synagogue was smashed. They were blindfolded and taken away in a wagon bed with no thought for comfort or convenience. They were told nothing and barely given bathroom breaks. Finally, they arrived at an old gate-house which was to become their first home. It was away from any real town, and they were separated, one with the children, one with the women, and the husband with the men. They would not see each other for two weeks, and when they did, it was from a distance.

That was when Abraham began spying on them from the woods. He was so relieved to find they had not already been taken to the quarry. He was part of a Jewish resistance group that had refused to wear stars or arm bands. Very early on, they had decided to leave their homes but could not get out of the country so they began to hide in the woods, and there they would run into each other soon forming an organization of sorts. They decided that they would forage in the woods for food and build shelters as a collective. They would steal food when necessary but most often took back belongings which they already owned, or which had been the possessions of their kidnapped friends. In this way, they survived and watched. When they could, they made contact with their imprisoned family and friends.

Abraham had made it his mission to rescue his aunt, uncle and cousin, and that was what they had just done. First, the family on the inside had to obtain jobs which would leave them in close proximity of each other during part of each day. Others were only too happy to allow them to collect trash throughout the dorms and deliver it to a dugout area in the woods but away from the river. The area they were in was on a large island in the river. They must be saved before being taken to the horrible quarry with its bone breaking jobs.

Previously, the trash from this area had been dumped into the Danube, but "the filth of these people must be buried" was a quote from a guard here that turned into law. In any case, the family used their duties to reconnect. And Abraham scouted out a path for them through the woods to a spot at which he would find a way to pick them up along the river. Escapes had been attempted previously but this was the first time a boat had been coordinated with the effort.

And it did pay off with the three family members joining the band in the woods; they would even find warm clothing rolled into bags for each of them. Likewise, Mojca and Vid made their way back to their hidden bags and then onto the train the next morning. They looked unkempt; however in these difficult times, they were not alone in showing the trials of the war on their person.

Julijana worried for three days regarding her sister's safety and whereabouts. She then received a telegram thanking her family for a wonderful visit and stating they were now proceeding with their plans. Hansi could not understand why she was so relieved, and she shrugged it off saying she was "afraid of everything during a war."

It would only be two months later that she heard a terrible tale at the open market. It seemed a young boy who used to assist one of the vendors was found face down floating in the Danube that morning. There was a bullet hole in the back of his head. The story circulated that he had been going up the river regularly trying to rescue Jewish prisoners, when he was caught. His boat had capsized the night before, and a group of guards had used him, some escapees, and their boat for target practice. It was whispered that this was quite a shame; the boy should not have been so foolish as to fail to comply with the rules.

23

WHERE ARE ALL THE CHILDREN?

As the war broke out, Rositha and Vilma were in London; Hansi, Julijana and Peter were relocating from Vienna to Linz where they hoped to be safe and of more help to the Reich; and Mojca and Vid were finalizing their plans as well. Vid had met and befriended several Slovenes who had become established in Australia soon after the Great War. The choice had been logical enough as the location of Australia gave it every prospect of being safe from bombings. The fact that it was an English-speaking country did not deter the Slovenes, as so many had learned English through American movies and music that they were comfortable with it and they believed the English to be fair-minded people. But the greatest influence on this exodus to Australia was that the United States had put immigration quotas into effect in 1920. Australia was still willing to accept all, and many feared a protracted wait for admission to the USA might lead to more troubles at home as they continued to wait for permission to enter.

Vid bought boat passage and committed himself to serve as a worker in the construction industry Down Under. House building was booming with the great influx of European citizens seeking a place to live far removed from war. There would soon be large clusters of Slovenians residing in Australia, missing home but feeling safe. These enclaves would grow even bigger at the end of WWII as Yugoslavians fled communism in their own country.

Once Vid and Mojca reached Australia, Vid wanted them to marry, but Mojca now considered herself a Bohemian and said she wished to live as man and wife but not be tied together by the Church. Her heart still stung from the disgraceful way she believed her sister was treated by the priest in Bled, and she did not want to put these men on a pedestal, or bow to them. She said, "We will work hard for our money and help those that we believe in and care for, but I do not need the Church in the middle to decide who gets what and how much they must keep for their trouble!"

And so, Vid, who loved her, accepted her terms and went on with a life where they would be devoted to each other and their future children but never look back as though the Church needed to be compensated for their choices. They were pioneers in a big and open land and would not visit their homeland again until after the reign of communism and Tito, were history. But, at the desperate request of Julijana, Mojca would ask to delay their trip just a few weeks and Vid would comply with her wishes, as he would always.

When Hitler took control of Austria, he set his sights on the Kingdom of Yugoslavia, among many smaller countries he wished to make his territory. But early on, Yugoslavia had declared itself neutral in this war, and members of the King's Royal Army were simply ordered to protect their home boundaries and the King. Peter I had died in 1921 to be followed by Alexander I who was murdered in Paris at a meeting. Since Alexander's son, Peter II, was so young, a cousin Paul was named Prince Regent who served as King and was dealing with the Reich. Through him a fateful error would be committed.

Many citizens of Yugoslavia were still angry that this Serbian monarchy had been forced upon them at the end of WWI. As WWII approached, resistance groups to this monarchy emerged taking the name of "Partisans." And as Paul was "friendly" with the Reich, they became increasingly certain that he would not fight the Nazis, thus their opposition to "The Royalists" increased. They considered non-Partisans as traitors. And, as WWII continued, the Russians left the Axis and joined in with the Allies. This helped to form a liaison with the Partisans who received strength and support from the Communist Russians. Tito, an Austrian Communist, took on leadership of the Partisans and added the lethal component of organization to the group. He ordered the Partisans to carry out security measures and to set up a Supreme Command with Partisan headquarters in each province. There were also "national liberation committees" in liberated areas that added strength to their security work.

So the Partisans opposed the Reich and were supported by the Allies. This meant that, within the confines of Yugoslavia, there were men running around in the woods hoping to kill the traitors who embraced the Germans. But because they were Communists, they also found those in the Church to be enemies. They also were opponents of the Royal Army of the Kingdom and wished to murder any that supported hierarchal thinking. They detested the notion of accumulated wealth which the King's forces appeared to represent. They labeled all who would not fight against the Nazis, as they fought, to be cowards. It was really a civil war going on, as World War II was breaking out in earnest in The Kingdom. Brother was literally fighting against brother, for the Partisans/Communists and the Royal Army members had often grown up in the same households.

As the war progressed, the Lovrenc family had no women left in The Kingdom of Yugoslavia except for Andrej Jr.'s wife, Marica, in Belgrade. His sisters had all left, and his mother had just passed away. His brother Ivan was about to marry, but he still remained on the farm. Due to his disability from the railroad because of a head injury, he was prevented from having to take sides in this war, and no army would enlist him. He helped his father and, when necessary, could row the pletna. They were just two to feed most nights so the effort required to survive was considerably diminished. Unfortunately, the same could be said for their quality of life, but under the circumstances, the two men did not complain and were glad to have each other's companionship.

It was Andrej, Jr. who faced the most immediate danger in the current situation. Having been raised as such a devout Catholic, he was not even able to consider the possibility of becoming a Communist Partisan. Many of his friends attempted to convince him that the Nazis must be opposed, that Hitler was a lunatic and that he not only was condemning Jews to death, but any who opposed Hitler. For example, Hitler decided that the Gypsies around the countryside were not of pure blood; therefore, they too, had to be interred in camps. But Andrej was following the Crown's orders to remain neutral and he could not see how this relieved him of his duties as a member of the Royal Army. He was steadfast, even when he experienced an attack by the Partisans that nearly took his life.

He and his men were conducting a scan of one of Yugoslavia's boundaries. The intent of this mission was to keep the country free of invaders on either side. A scout from Andrej's group had detected a campfire up ahead, about a kilometer from them, along the same woodland path. Knowing that Partisans were up ahead gave them a great advantage. They fell back slightly to regroup and then to rush forward planning to overwhelm the enemy. These woodland attacks were a major part of the civil war.

The King's men banded tightly together but in a formation which would allow them to peel apart at the last moment and instantly have use of their weapons, at which point they would separate and surround the enemy. The group, adrenalin flowing, started down the trail headed toward the lighted fire. Suddenly, from all sides, they heard a "whoop" and then the cry, "Death to traitors!" And they were fired upon from all sides by men hiding in the trees, and fell into a heap of blood and bones.

From the tangled, tortured, pile of bodies there emitted loud sounds of moaning and sharp cries of pain. Since the shooting had stopped, the group lay in total, sticky, darkness. Two men, as though they had been coated in lard, slithered their way out of the mess of dead and dying and disappeared into the deep underbrush just as the Partisans reached the trail from their shooting blinds in the woods. One narrowly missed stepping on the crawling escapees.

But, two escapees there were. And one of the escapees was Andrej, covered in blood from other soldiers' wounds and grazed by two bullets; he was nevertheless intact and able to get his fellow soldier to a safe place to bind his wounds. They rested for a few hours. When they were certain that no one else from their party had survived and should be helped, and that the Partisans had gone in the opposite direction, they made their way back to the barracks, where yet another Partisan trick was reported and recorded.

Andrej thought, "I shall remember that if it looks too easy, it is probably a trap. These Partisans grew up in the woods as did most of us. They know where all the trails go, where the climbs are too steep, and where there are abandoned buildings which would be good for hiding. They also know when it is a bad time to show firelight. If I don't take them for fools, they will not be able to make a fool out of me."

24

ANDREJ AND GUARDING HIS HOME

L ife went on, even in the midst of war. With all the unspeakable horror, death, and tragedies in the concentration camps, still, babies were born, although survival rates were not good. In other areas of the war, soldiers helped to conceive babies wherever they were stationed. Many people fell in love and love was heightened by the backdrop of drama. That is, if girl meets boy during non-war times, there is a tendency to take one's time in escalating the romance. Sex was delayed to keep a man interested, or because one's values did not condone such behavior outside of marriage, at least during this period. Also, in ordinary times, there were traditional rituals such as getting to know the family and friends of the beloved. And, although men were always anxious to conquer women, both parties tended not to rush things, especially if they could foresee the possibility of a serious future together.

But, during a war, if two people fall in love, there is a sense of desperation not to let the beloved get away; the relationship should not disintegrate simply because the soldier must follow orders to move on. A man could plead for love based on that old cliché, "For tomorrow I may die!" And women found this difficult to deny. So there were many relationships which came together quickly during the war years, even if the beloved were a member of the opposition country. Such is the nature of need and attraction.

In Andrej's case, he saw his new bride frequently as he was a member of the Royal Army, and often at home or living near her as she was just outside of the city of Belgrade. They had many happy nights together although he fought to downplay the fears he had over the "jungle warfare" he found each time he had to go out on patrol. He did not mention the booby traps and the continual anger of the Partisans lurking about the countryside. As a member of the King's Army, he had to fight his former friends and neighbors who wished to see Yugoslavia under Communist control and fight any foreign enemy attempting to defile Yugoslavia's neutrality. The influence which the Partisans fell under from the Communist Party by way of the Red or Russian Army was both an internal problem and one of outside influence. This was no course for the man who loved God and country. The priests, from the pulpits, were condemning the Partisans to death, leaving a man like Andrej with his moral compass spinning. He could only vow to try and keep his country safe from this Partisan influence and do as his king ordered.

He followed orders and prayed his king was in the right. That the king and the priests were in agreement gave Andrej at least a sense that the Royal Army continued to be the course he must follow. And when Marica became pregnant in 1939, Andrej was overjoyed. This was the news he needed to keep himself strong and faithful to the cause he had pursued. With many friends claiming that he "was a coward" for not fighting against the Monarchy, he needed to believe that his action on behalf of country and king was a noble one; he needed to believe his decisions were right and just. As a good Catholic, he saw the baby as proof from God that he was doing the right thing by protecting the home and the decisions of the king.

But when his little girl, Valerija, was born in 1940, he would have only a brief time to get to know and treasure her. He thought of the night of her birth as a slice of perfection: he had his wife, baby girl, beloved dog and the time to hold them all. Yet, the tide of the war was changing, and Yugoslavia would be caught in the middle. Perhaps sensing this, the couple laughed and played with the baby at every opportunity. Andrej seemed to want to provide her with a lifetime of love within a few months. He knew that things were getting worse for his men: more ambushes were taking their lives; more had been caught in bloody gun battles with the well supplied Partisans. Then Paul, King Regent, made his terrible mistake.

Paul did not comprehend the value his people had placed on neutrality, or their general preference for the British and the Allies. Certainly, he was pressured by Adolf Hitler and perhaps promised rewards for their supposed success. On March 25, 1941, he made a decision to sign a Tripartite Pact stating that Yugoslavia would be "a friend to Nazi Germany and her Axis of power." The people of Yugoslavia erupted against their Regent.

There arose in the Kingdom such an enormous outcry against Paul, and what he stood for, that it opened the door for a bloodless coup d'état which was orchestrated by a pro-British group. Peter II, who had just turned seventeen, was then declared King on March 27, two days after the Pact had been signed by Paul. The regent's guards saluted Peter II as their sovereign and thousands of pro-Allied Forces citizens, along with some British and French troops, were there to wave flags honoring him. Many organizations rejoiced, and it appeared that the political tide was overflowing in favor of this move toward the Allied Forces. The Partisans and King's Army alike rejoiced.

However, Hitler had other ideas and was furious with this change. He postponed an attack which he had planned in order to simultaneously attack Yugoslavia and Greece on April 6, 1941, ten days after Peter II became King. The Luftwaffe bombed Belgrade killing as many as 4,000 people. There was fighting in the streets and hundreds of prisoners were captured by the Germans as they fought to protect their homeland. Partisans and the Royal Army fought together against these forces with the desire to drive them back to Germany. Then, suddenly, the Royal Army no longer had a King in power as the Germans forced Peter II out of his country, and he would "rule in exile" from several locations during the remainder of the war as supported by the Allies. In the first few days of Peter's exile, his army fought simply to guard their homes and to stand up for the will of the people.

It was in this sea of turmoil that Andrej was arrested, placed in shackles as a prisoner of war, and thrown into the back of a smelly, old truck which might have been commandeered from a pig farm. The truck would transport him over three days' worth of bumpy miles. He crossed through waterways with the truck floating on a barge and along twisting mountain passages which were barely accessible. Occasionally, he was offered water and a bathroom break, but food was only permitted once per day.

Andrej was now a prisoner of Nazi Germany. Nighttime was the worst time. When there was no light coming through the tarp on his truck, he would think about Marica, the baby and even his sweet dog. How dear his child was and how loving his wife and all the special meals she still had tried to prepare for him even though they were on rations. She did this because he was a soldier and must fight for his country and because he was her dearest husband, now the father of their precious baby girl. Cooking for him, she had said, was her part of the war effort and permitted her to give something to him when he was so exhausted. He repeated in his head, "I will come back to you, my love for our lives have only just begun, and we must be together for that darling Valerija and to give her a baby brother, God willing. I will fight to remain alive and well for the promise of holding you both in my arms again. And he remained stoic on the difficult trip in the back of a crowded truck, not knowing what lay ahead for him or where he was going. He wanted to memorize every bump along the way so he would recognize the path back knowing that would be a happy day.

When he arrived at the camp, he discovered that he was in Vienna. He wondered how far away his sisters might be; were Julijana, Peter and Hansi still in the city, or had the fighting forced them to move? Also, was Mojca still in this area? He had heard nothing from or about them since the war had started in earnest. He hoped that they had all found safety somewhere else, yet it also comforted him to think that he might see one of them pass by if they lived here. How he longed for the days of hiding on the pletna with Mojca and laughing when his toy gun had frightened the vandals. It brought another smile to his face. Someday, perhaps, he could take Valerija for a boat ride; that would be a true gift.

Once the soldiers were settled into what passed for barracks, the treatment became harsh. The German guards mocked them citing their worshiping of a king as foolish, and their neutrality with respect to the Jews as even more foolish. The only Jews that Andrej knew ran a lovely butcher shop in Belgrade where they had been able to purchase fine meat before the war was underway. He knew nothing of difficulty or ill treatment from them. He was a Catholic and would not harm his neighbor. The Lord, Jesus Christ, was a Jew. How could these Germans think so badly of them? But they wanted information, and they kept after him thinking that the big lapels on his coat meant that he had knowledge. All they meant was that he was permitted to carry arms just as they all were, now that the war was upon them.

His soldiers were cold at night, for Austria had harsh winters as she rested on the edge of the Alps. And the rooms they were kept in were not intended for the number of people that they held. Perhaps with fans on some days and a blanket on others, they might have found some comfort, but, as it was, most nights they must shiver themselves to sleep. Still, Andrej warmed himself through his heart. He thought about his wife and daughter. Was Valerija walking yet and if she might now say Mama? Would she remember him? Had Marica been able to get word to his father and Ivan that he had been taken? Was his family in Slovenia doing alright?

It was impossible to know, but he vowed to handle whatever questions and abuse were demanded of him. He would eat what was provided even if he could see worms in the wheat gruel, and the milk had gone sour. He needed the sustenance, and he would survive. Thus, the good man he had always been continued to shine through; he did not complain, he did not argue, he did not make trouble. At every opportunity he served as a good example for his men. He showed tolerance, a stoic nature and bravery. They could all put up with a few rough days to be free at the end of this terrible war. He was going home again, he knew it.

25

HOMESICK DURING THE WAR

One thing Rositha and Vilma had not counted on was becoming homesick just as Europe was gearing up for war. They had finally both found jobs, a secure place in which to live, and were making friends but, Vilma especially, was constantly talking about Slovenia. "Do you remember mother's wild strawberry jam?" she would say, or "The jam tarts she would always make this time of year?" Or, "Don't you think that the sunset on Lake Bled is the prettiest thing you've ever seen?"

And by then, Rositha had to confess that she did miss all these things, and even their mother who sometimes had ruled with a wooden spoon if the girls got fresh, or wanted to skip chores. So Vilma and Rositha planned to take a long weekend trip home. They would travel with only a backpack each, making it easy to walk on and off transportation and providing little to be scrutinized by customs.

Naturally, everyone was happy to see them, and then they were asked to assist with the chores which were only natural. But as soon as she was able, Vilma headed into the village. It seemed that a man who was now managing the postal service, thus not being drafted, was still very interested in Vilma. They had actually confessed their love for each other while on a "farewell" date as the girls prepared to leave for London. His name was Sveto, and they had first met in school, but had largely ignored each other until recently. He was nice looking and had grown tall in his late teens.

Now, with Vilma only available for the weekend, he was determined that she should know his full feelings. He proposed to her on this short trip home and wanted to speak with her family. This created quite a stir, but Vilma did feel she owed it to Rositha, and to the family for whom she worked, to take a little time before any date should be set. After all, Andrej had just gotten married and Rositha was counting on her partnership for survival in London. So, with great longing in their eyes Sveto and Vilma parted tearfully at the railway station and the girls then made their trek back to London.

The hall phone rang for Vilma as they were unpacking their backpacks back at their boarding house. It was her cousin Manca. Manca, filled with robust importance, could not turn her head when she learned of the grave injustice which was about to occur between Sveto and Vilma. Did Vilma think that Sveto had just been counting posies while she was away? Manca said, "Vilma you should know that he has been seriously interested in other women when you are gone, in fact, he and Zala have a baby on the way! I have heard it from several friends!"

This was the first devastating shock a man would give Vilma. She could barely reply to her cousin and almost accused her of not wanting to see her happy, but she relented and took in the words as well as the outcome this behavior left her to make. She had to draw a sad conclusion. Vilma knew she would not want a man who had been both sneaky and dishonest with her. Yet, she thought of his handsome face and wondered how she could ever live without him.

She waited a few days until the pain had somewhat subsided; she asked Rositha if she thought Sveto was marrying material, knowing full well Rositha would not put up with any foolishness. Then, through cascades of tears, she wrote a letter and told her beloved to do the right thing and marry the woman whom he had impregnated; and to leave her alone, that she would never marry him.

After enough time had elapsed for her letter to have been delivered, she received a phone call from Sveto's sister telling Vilma of his suicide by gunshot; there was no going back.

Vilma tried to be strong, but her emotions pulled her in diverging directions. Part of the time she was consumed with guilt over his loss, part of the time she was angry with him for throwing his life away in this manner, and at other times she felt she had escaped a terrible fate by not ending up married to such a man. She remained much unsettled for weeks, and then her employers announced that her services were no longer needed as they were fleeing to the United States out of fear of the war. They were fortunate in that they found an uncle who would sponsor them.

Now Vilma had no boyfriend and no job. Just as despair was about to overwhelm her, she received an invitation to interview for a new nanny position. At this interview she found that she would be working for a countryman, a Serbian diplomat, his wife, and child. They would be stationed in Belgrade. Although she had planned on leaving Yugoslavia until the war was over, she decided to take this risk since the life she had planned had collapsed around her.

In a matter of weeks she was leaving Rositha behind in London while she traveled with the Serbian family. Rositha was busy working for the Wedgwoods and did not oppose her sister's change of plans. And Vilma felt safe in the fact that Andrej and Marica, lived in Belgrade, and she would be living with the diplomat's family.

However, the best laid plans have difficulty providing an adequate crystal ball during war times, and Velma wasn't long in Yugoslavia's capital before Belgrade crowned a young king and was then the battle ground for Hitler's rage on those who did not follow his edicts. Belgrade was under attack from the air and on the ground just two weeks after Peter II was elevated to King. While her brother, Andrej, was fighting for the King and for his own life, Vilma was frantically packing bags for the diplomat and his family, as they obtained special passage out of Yugoslavia and on to Greece.

Once in Greece, the ship was soon turned away as German troops were invading there as well. Next, their ship, the SS Strathaird, a cruise ship that had been converted to a troop ship during the war, took them from Crete to Egypt. They were welcomed to debark in Egypt and treated initially like tourists. Vilma was frightened by the enormity of the pyramids and the antiquity which she judged to be an unsafe combination. Thus, while others were touring the ancient ruins, she was waiting outside lest the buildings should collapse.

Her reluctance to enter the tomb of "the gods" had a side effect other than missing an opportunity to see this great wonder. While she awaited her party, she observed a gathering which included people who seemed to be from the press. They were just down a large staircase from where Vilma sat fanning herself with a hat. As they drew closer, Vilma was certain that she saw the new boy king being toured about the pyramids. Not wishing to miss this, she attempted to draw closer and was suddenly questioned by two armed men. Later she would suppose they might have taken her for a German but at the time she was able to produce her papers and prove she was one of this man's subjects, although far from home.

She was allowed to get close enough to have a good look at Peter II, and when he glanced her way, she executed the loveliest of curtseys, one which would have made her mother proud. She was sure he waved to her from his entourage, and this remained a highlight of her world travel experiences.

But the heat was so intense in Cairo that Vilma threw caution to the wind and indulged in swimming in a public place. Once they were back on board ship and headed for Cape Town, Vilma became very ill. It was always assumed that she did not have the immunities for the water in Egypt. Fortunately, she recovered, but Egypt and Cape Town, which they found a lovely place, would also not grant them asylum. They then made the long journey to Rio de Janeiro and then on to New York City.

In New York Harbor they were again denied asylum. There seemed to be too many refugees for any of these countries to wish to give them space and support. After a few days of regrouping, and with much trepidation, the decision had to be made to cross the Atlantic; The United Kingdom had agreed to take them in. They proposed to enhance their odds of survival by adding some sister ships to their fleet so that they would not face the high seas alone. The problem was that it had taken several months for them to reach this point of action, and the Atlantic was by now a big part of the war grounds. They would face U-boats, enemy war craft, submarines loaded with torpedoes, and possible air strikes.

Once their ship was out just beyond Canada the rules for the passengers changed. There was to be no frivolity in the evenings, nothing that would require lighting. As darkness fell, they were essentially prisoners within their ship. They each had small low powered flashlights for nocturnal trips to the loo, but only if they could absolutely not use moonlight by which to see. In this way, each person must be accountable for the safety of all.

The more heroic requirement involved the ships. These large vessels motoring through the night were not permitted to have their lights on. The moon would reveal each sister ship's shape to the other vessels, but not every night was moonlit. And the hope was that no recognizance flights would spot this cluster of ships floating through the moonlight. If they could be discovered by the planes, then their locations would be radioed to the ships, or submarines, waiting to block their progress by blowing them out of the water.

Vilma found this silence, and the absence of needed light, to be terrifying. There was only so much talking in the dark that one could handle before eliminating most meaningful conversation. Then individuals would either drink too much or retire for the evening. Usually, that was the route that Vilma took so long as the diplomat's daughter did not require her services. Then Vilma would lie on her bed and listen.

She thought by carefully monitoring each sound she could somehow prevent a catastrophe from happening; as though her ears, and her will to live, would keep bombs from landing on them, or torpedoes from flying through the deep, dark, blue sea and crushing their hulls. Then she dreamed of the ocean roaring in on them where they would either freeze to death in lifeboats, or be eaten by sharks, if they did not immediately drown. Another terrifying option would be their invisibility and therefore being run over by the big ships which could not see to rescue them.

As an alternative to her fear of the attack, she would travel down the self-recrimination slide and think of what she should have done to save her relationship with Sveto. She now reasoned he must truly have loved her and could not bear the pain of her loss; when she had denied him the promise of matrimony, he was too bereft to continue living. Perhaps he had made a single drunken mistake with the woman who was pregnant and was simply not suited to a life with her or her with him. If only Manca hadn't told her that he was in trouble, they could be happily married at that moment, instead of her being tossed about the sea in a blackened state of terror which reminded her of a floating coffin.

And then one of their ships was torpedoed, and, as it occurred, they did not know how badly it had been hit, or how much more fire they would be taking. The noise was not noticeable until it struck stealthily from underwater as fired by a submarine. Jumping up and peering out her porthole, Vilma could see one of the other ships shaking and soon lurching. She did not know what to do but hurried to the next berth to see how her charge was. The girl's parents were already with her and advised Vilma not to panic. They must remain calm to assess what the damage was and to listen for announcements from the Captain.

Eventually they were to discover that several deaths had occurred. But the vessel was surprisingly not lost, and passengers from the damaged section were transferred to another ship as soon as there was daylight. Here, the surviving passengers spoke of a moment when the moonlight allowed them to see the great white light of the torpedo rushing through the water and heading directly at their ship. It was as though a great white shark was coming for each of them. They cried out in terror while repeating their tale. When the entire fleet managed to complete the trip to England without further incident all knew they had been extremely lucky. But, Vilma could only repeat after this heroic voyage that she would never again board a ship. She kept that promise.

26

UNDER FIRE BY YOUR ALLIES

While Andrej was determined to survive his captivity, no matter what it entailed, things did not get any easier. In actuality, everything continued on a steep decline. It was like the jump off a bridge where the bungee cord will probably save you, but the bottom is unclear, and you are pepper sprayed at every level. Yet, while in the air you still remain unsure if, at the end, you will swing back into a ledge.

Right from the start there was too little food, and it was provided sporadically. To these farmers turned soldiers, it resembled quality as poor as the slop they would have fed to their pigs. Many times, Andrej would say to his men, trying to force some levity into his voice, "Just hold your nose and dive in. No need to waft the enticing fumes your way, simply engage your mouth and disengage your sense of smell!" And then he would lead by example, wolfing the meal down as quickly as he could not to prolong the flavor or the decision making. The less time the food spent on his tongue, the better the probability he could take another bite. Once you had accepted that you would consume this meal, you were best off doing so without hesitation.

The only trick which remained then was getting out of sight of the food fast enough that nothing you could see, or inhale, would cause the meal to jump back up your throat and exit. This would undo the benefit of the whole exercise which was to remain alive.

Andrej employed some additional strategies to assist him in surviving each day. He had formulated what he thought of as "mind support." He had several vignettes that all concerned the possibility of escaping, which he told himself to be prepared for at any time. In some, he found a way to bribe a guard, although he had absolutely no money, and his wedding ring had been stolen early on. Still, this didn't keep the thought from being a comfort.

In others, he happened upon a sleeping guard, or a drunken one, and this allowed him to access the outside world without being watched. But his favorite fantasy, and one he told himself nearly every night to help him fall asleep, was that Mojca or Julijana happened to be walking by the camp. He saw her and tossed little pebbles her way until she looked up and ran over to his position against a fence. They had a few minutes to form a plan which Julijana's husband would help to execute. He posed as a Nazi officer and demanded the release of Andrej to be his servant. Later that night, he and his sisters and their families would escape over the mountains back to Yugoslavia. This became one of his favorite day dreams.

It was an amazing coincidence that there was then a period of time when his captors decided that the stronger men could be of use to them. Of course they didn't want to introduce the possibility of sabotage, or escape, but they needed men to clean up after the bombings. Small work parties would be sent into the areas which had just been bombed. Vienna was being hit hard by the Allies to keep oil from being distributed. The Nazi party could get the damage out of the way faster and do what was necessary for reconstruction, if they forced the prisoners into labor. And that is what they did. Many of the captives were strong farm boys, so, with an improvement in caloric intake, they were useable as work animals. This certainly caused resentment and demoralization as the prisoners were asked to undo the damage they had rejoiced in seeing occur, but at least it enabled them to be guaranteed their next meal.

It was a strange feeling to be cheering on the inside when you knew the "good guys" were flying overhead and blasting the ground around you, while simultaneously hoping that you could survive the barrage. Yet, the angrier the Germans were, the better the POWs felt but could never express this. When the United States was also participating in the bombing, it was a sign that the war was not going in the direction which the Germans had planned. It also was at a time when the German, Italian, and Japanese forces were spread thin, close to the point where Italy would turn her weapons over to the Russians strengthening those forces, which included the Partisans, but were fighting the Nazis. Yes, the Communists fought against the Nazis, but they brought along their own forces of evil which would remain in Yugoslavia for a long period of time.

And, as the Germans became more spread out in battles, and were more regularly defeated, their troops were dying of the cold and starvation. Certainly, food for prisoners, never previously a priority, was not now a consideration. In this half-starved state, Andrej had numerous crazy ideas. Many were escape fantasies where he could magically sneak by the guards under the darkened sky, and get far enough away by morning to avoid detection as an escapee.

But one day, his escape fantasy ran into a possible avenue towards this goal. While he and a crew were positioned well away from the camp cleaning up after a recent bombardment, he recognized the street name on which they were working. Over the last few years, he had written several times to Julijana, and sent some funny pictures he liked to draw, to little Peter. They were mostly dogs or other animals with smiles on their faces. And that day they were working on Wunder Strasse, and 789 Wunder Strasse had been his sister's address. His heart beat rapidly thinking that perhaps she was just a few feet away. Could he find her without being observed and hide in her basement? Could this be an early ticket out of the prison camp? Andrej could hardly contain himself. He started reading all the house numbers, quickly discovering the direction he must go to reach her apartment. The street was so badly torn up that there were men working at varying locations.

Slowly, Andrej joined a nearby crew in the area he wished to be near, then another one a little closer, and so on, until he was at her precise location. Here his heart sank with such a dive he felt there would be holes under his feet where it had buried itself into the depth of the soil. The apartment building which had been seated at this spot was splintered and fractured into thousands of pieces. There were glass fragments sparkling everywhere, as though it had been raining prisms. There was even a crater where the building's cellar had once offered support to the rooms above. The pieces which had once been the dwelling were vaporized or scattered over several city blocks and streets. This recent bombing would have killed any occupants. He stared at the sight not even aware that he was doing so; long enough that it attracted a guard's attention.

"You got a problem with doing your job prisoner 70893?" he heard.

Quickly Andrej remembered that survival was his goal, and he could not be caught mourning something that was already finished.

He could grieve later when he was alone, or perhaps imagine that they had all, somehow, made it to safety. "No Sergeant!" he replied and went on shoveling rocks and debris. The few tears on his cheek would not be observed, and he would continue his personal mission some other way. He only prayed that his sister and nephew were safe somewhere else, and one day they could laugh about this. For the first time in weeks, he repeated prayers he had learned as a Catholic boy. These images of God and Jesus were the only comfort available to him, and he had to place his faith in God to get through those next few hours.

Once he had suffered through the evening meal, he retired to bed as soon as possible. Ordinarily the men would sit around for a while hoping someone could tell a story to jolly them along. They were permitted to have contact with each other so long as it was out in the open. No one was permitted to have private conversations or private contact. But that night Andrej remarked on the difficulty of the day's labor and went to bed. The men in the labor details were permitted the use of cots while all the others slept in hammocks or on the ground. At least Andrej could be alone for a few precious hours and there he did more praying for his sisters whom he presumed might well be dead. And he always prayed for his wife and his darling baby daughter, and sometimes even for his dog Kam. Each prayer contained a promise that he hoped God was listening to as he told himself that he would hold them again. Then he would amplify all the messages he fed himself saying to carry on, and live through each day, even when the bombs were close by.

He visualized watching baby Valerija as she first learned to feed herself with her little arms in the air and her fists clenching and unclenching in excitement as she signaled for more food. Her shy and sly look when she placed too much food in her mouth and still swallowed it down, checking to see who was watching her. And then her chortles of utter joy when her parents would clap their hands, and she clapped hers, to demonstrate her successful completion of the meal; after these thoughts Andrej could then sleep.

The next day his crew had to return to the same area in which he knew Julijana had lived. Here he spotted a red scrap of material under some fallen columns. The material was similar to a color his mother and the girls had once dyed some of their wool from which they had then made caps. They had used this color to make the material more Christmas-like, for the hats were given as gifts the year before the war had broken out. All of them, males and females alike, had received a bright red chapeau, for, in addition to being decorative, the color enhanced their safety, as they lived so close to the forest. It was not unheard of for accidental shootings to occur, especially if the victim had brown hair and was taken for a deer. By getting into the habit of wearing these caps, Justa used to believe she was keeping her family from harm. She always told them that she spun the wool with extra love, said a prayer over the loom, and kissed the final product.

Andrej wondered if this toque could have attracted a bomber. He worked his way over to the swatch of red and could not decide what to do. He wasn't certain if he wanted to take it with him or bury it. In the end, just as he was about to walk away, he swooped down and brought the scrap up to his neck dropping it down in his shirt to rest close to his heart.

27

CONTINUING TO SURVIVE
UNTIL THE END

Every person has a breaking point; a place which, once crossed, makes their lives unbearable, even though their will to survive had once been strong. In dogs, researchers would call it learned helplessness triggered by repeatedly shocking animals and denying them any reward. That was a good summary of what life was like for Andrej, for along that route to survival he needed something to reinforce his value for life. They had removed him from all the people he loved, taken away his personal dignity, kept him from obtaining basic needs such as a palatable meal and a good night's sleep, and now they had taken a large chip out of his hope. While, perhaps, he could not blame the Nazis for this last loss, as it was their territory which had been destroyed by Allied bombers, still it was the mad aggression of their leader which put all of them in harm's way. He now had to think that his oldest sister, who had often acted in the role of their mother, had been blown to pieces amidst the shards of stone, wood, and glass which he and his group had been shoveling.

The rubble was so pulverized that much of it would remain unrecognizable, as some was actually returned to ashes. He could decipher some of the matter, such as pieces of glass or bone fragments, but what was in the fine dust would have to wait several decades and chemical analysis to be identified. Every crack and crevice in his face retained some of this grit. Sometimes he would sneeze and then have the grizzly thought, had he just expelled some of Julijana? Thinking of her as perhaps dead beneath his feet in the gray and crumbling debris was unfathomable.

It was tragic to see fellow soldiers meet their end, but to think of his lovely sister in this way was for him nearly the worst of imaginable pain. Yet, that slight qualification, that there was something worse he might imagine, and that was the death of his beautiful wife and his darling Valerija, began to bring him back into fighting form. So long as he had reasonable hope that they still lived, he would shake off the pain and fight his way back. It took several weeks after the discovery of the red hat, to which he intended to hold on forever, before he could again eat and demonstrate any resiliency, but his spirit returned. However, the war continued on, and the lack of provisions led to far less food for the prisoners, most civilians, and all but the elite in the Nazi regime.

The prisoners' continued discomfort led to them attempting to scrounge scraps found in trash bins that they would pass by while performing clean-up duty. Most of what had been tossed out was inedible but it didn't stop starving men from trying. Conversations, when they had any, always quickly reverted to the theme of food, what their wives often cooked, what they grew in their gardens back home, and their own recipes for venison sausage. They had taken to "souping," which was the art of adding water to any food which was provided, so that it appeared to be more, and they could make it last longer. Still, the water did not enhance the caloric intake.

Additionally, the cold was worse because they were not well fed and because their clothing was worn even thinner over time. If they found a scrap of material, paper, or cardboard, these were fashioned in some manner to wrap around their bodies so that their clothing served as a second or third layer. And a solid piece of cardboard would be placed inside of boots as the soldier prayed for just a little protection for his feet. Foot sores, and painful and bleeding feet were complaints now equal to the agony of hunger.

No one in the group died with good boots on, but there was a natural rush to inspect any footwear which was left behind by the dead. Typically, if the shoes had any wear left in them, they would have been confiscated by the Reich before the lowly POWs were permitted to bury their dead. But, if a POW did receive even the scraps of someone's boots, the pieces might be used to reinforce their own footwear, or more humbly turned into soup. These desperate fellows had learned that boiling leather for a prolonged period of time would tenderize it and release some flavor into the water. They had no idea what toxins might also be released, but, if they could add a bit of salt and perhaps some grease to the water, they would relish the concoction as manna.

The Nazis were, in fact, famously known for recycling human excrement onto their gardens during this period to see if it would enhance plant growth the way that cow and horse manure did. There were those among the scientific minded who were also suspected of believing that decomposing human bodies might make fine fertilizer. The POWs were anxious to bury their own before they would watch their friend fading away as he decomposed on some flowering plants in the German officers' section. It seemed to them that the Reich must have totally lost their sense of smell, so disgusting were these two practices of fertilizing plants. Andrej had never seen a body in a garden, but some of his men were so disturbed at this point in time that they swore the behavior occurred.

They all started hating the enemy even more than they had at the time of their original captivity. Familiarity did, indeed, breed contempt. This was a natural evolution given the indignities to which the POWs were continuously exposed, but it led to an exacerbation of dangerous behavior by the POWs. Men were more challenging of the Reich's soldiers and, therefore, more likely to be in trouble with their captors. And punishments led to even poorer conditions for those fellows who had demonstrated their disgust. After months together, the Germans now understood more of their captives' vocabulary and did not appreciate the words used to describe them. Certainly, tensions mounted in a manner quite the opposite of the Stockholm effect, where captives and captors, over time, start to see each other as more human with more ideology in common.

Andrej thought about his family and continued to write home whether or not there was any chance that the letters would be delivered. The act of writing was like highlighting a contract he had made within himself to carry on for the hope of holding them again in his arms. On the mornings after he had written home, he was a stronger and more determined man. He put the red cap inside his breast pocket, wrapped himself in two layers of cardboard scraps, and marched to duty with his head held as high as he could muster, even though he was cold and starving. He was, in his heart, still a member of the Royal Army of the Kingdom of Yugoslavia, and he could not act as less.

Some of the men had begun trapping cats, or even rats, they did not much care which, so long as there were a few ounces of meat to be gleaned from the carcass. If a cat were pregnant, there were men who could feast upon the grizzly fetuses, while others became almost sentimental about "poor kittens." It no longer amazed Andrej to observe a man seeming to be profoundly touched by the death of the animals but still enjoying kitten stew. Such were the extremes in which men were placed during war and these were the good guys.

He often thought of the extreme behaviors of the German soldiers. By now, many knew what was going on inside those camps. They were not simply forced labor camps but houses of horror and death. And their own emaciation was apparently nothing by comparison to these poor, terrorized Jews. "Good Germans" had complained of the distaste they felt when realizing that the ashes raining down on them were cremains; the ashes of human bodies. Yet, their disgust was not applied to the logical conclusion that, for there to be ash, then thousands, even millions, had to have perished, and what complaints did they make about that?

He could not conceive of the typical low-level guard, perhaps a man with a family nearby, who would go home at night and say to his kin: "Just an ordinary day at the crematorium." or "I cannot tell you how many children we barbequed today." Andrej, with his strong family values, his Catholic upbringing, and his joy around people and children, found this Reich the most revolting thing he could imagine. He awakened in cold sweats most nights, by a panic equally terrifying as his fear of loss of family, and that was his utter frustration with not being free to fight this war. That he must clean up for these animals, and not fight against them.

This is when his escape fantasy took on a new shape – one of revenge!

28

A CHANCE FOR ROMANCE
IN THE WAR

Rositha had been concerned about the war in a more personal way than simply surviving and praying for the troops. Certainly, everyone was consumed with concern for those who must fight, for the millions of persecuted and starving, and those, like her brother Andrej, whom she knew was a Nazi POW. She lived and prayed through many bombings there in London, with friends and children crying in terror. But whenever she had time to do the mathematics of the situation, women her age were at a particular disadvantage. She had left Slovenia just before the war broke out and was twenty-six years old in 1938. The custom of the times was that a single woman of her age was likely never to bear children and was referred to as a spinster.

Rositha had always loved little children. She enjoyed their innocence and playfulness and loved to see them develop with encouragement. She had been certain that the time would come for her to be a mother. But, during her years in Slovenia, the right man had never happened by. She had met a few men but always felt they were waiting for some war to be over, or for the economy to change; the time was never right. Now she was over thirty, and still the war raged on. Perhaps she would have to take this blind date with the American soldier more seriously.

The soldier apparently had leave this coming Saturday and hoped to meet her in front of the bus stop which he thought was near her apartment. It wasn't simply near her apartment, it was next to it, so that all she had to do was to look out the window, and the gentleman would be facing her window just twelve feet away. It was the perfect place for her to obtain a little recognizance to see whom she was meeting. Their rendezvous was scheduled for two P.M. so that they might ride together to the park on a bus which was still operating, walk about for a bit, and then select a spot for dinner.

Rositha had gone to great lengths to prepare her hair and even wore one of her precious pairs of hosiery for the event. She had tried on all three of her good dresses in an attempt to determine which outfit would make her appear youngest. This was the gentleman for whom she had decided to change her birth date, as he was three years her junior, and for whom she wished to be a total of six years younger than her actual age. Yet, after all that preparation, when she gazed out the window she did not like what she saw. He was barely her height, wore glasses, and his hair was already thinning!

This may not have been a very gracious evaluation on her part, but she had built up her expectation of what this "Mr. Right" might look like. She thought that American soldiers would be tall, dark and handsome; not average height, simply cute, and balding. Whether right, or wrong of her, she decided not to start something she would not want to finish. She went back to her room and changed into a house dress.

Thirty minutes later, her curiosity got the better of her, and she glanced out the window. The soldier was still standing there and appeared not to have moved a muscle. She quickly ducked back down and went to another part of the building. She was a little restless at this point, but her curiosity continued to mount. Another thirty minutes passed and he was still standing at the bus stop, although he was now leaning in from the other side. "Holy Mother of God," she said actually blaspheming out loud, "what is wrong with that fool?" Then she went away for another 30 minutes, but when she looked again he was still there! "All right, all right!" she said as she ran down the hall and changed back into her nice outfit, grabbed her coat and handbag and ran for the bus stop.

"There you are," the soldier said beaming, "I knew you must have gotten tied up somehow and would make it."

She was at a loss to say much except "I am so happy that you waited for me." And thus began their first date.

As they walked though Hyde Park, he asked about her family in the Slovenian part of Yugoslavia. "Your English is very good," he added.

"Vell," she said, "my sister and I studied English before ve came here. But even so, many people think ve are Germans and I vant nothing to do vith that crazy Hitler!"

Hyde Park had changed significantly since the onset of the war. On good days, if no bombs had recently been dropped, there were folding chairs set up and a mixture of people sitting and taking in the sights. This was normal. But bombs were dropped in the park, and the military, by the next morning, would have organized clean-up crews. There were even bomb shelters in the park so that a wise visitor could keep the shelter's location in mind if they needed to make a hasty retreat to its cover.

THE RED TOQUE

The Park no longer particularly concerned itself with landscaping but more resembled a military post. Ninety percent of those strolling in the area were wearing uniforms, and many of these were women who were managing safety issues. When Rositha and Bernard strolled through the park, his uniform blended right in with the others, and they both made it a point to mention the shelter's location. It was not a quiet arboretum walk, but, as was typical of all walks once the Blitz had begun, it offered a chance to see others and to become accustomed to destruction and peace existing in harmony.

Bernard Adams, for that was his name, said "I admire your attitude. I come from a place in the States where people are very independent thinkers, and I believe the scenery is much like Slovenia. It is called Vermont. We have beautiful snow-capped mountains much of the year and pretty lakes with lots of trees in between."

"Yes," she answered, "that sounds wery much like Slowenia. And I am glad your state begins with a V as it will give me more practice to say it." And then they both laughed.

She told him about the lake they had lived near and also the beautiful ancient castle. There were many churches in Vermont, he said, but no real antiquity.

Bernard said, "I repair plane engines, so wherever the pilots and planes go, I must go too. It is good that I am mechanical so that the equipment will run well."

"And what do you do when the pilots are out shooting or bombing?" she asked.

"My buddy and I find broken down motorcycles, fix them up and see how far we can get before we must come back."

"Do you usually get them running?" she asked.

"Yes." was his answer, "Unless they've run over a land mine, then we move on."

It turned out to be a very pleasant afternoon and evening. Rositha felt a little disappointed when Bernard respectfully brought her back to her apartment building and did not "try anything." But then he asked, "What hours are you off tomorrow? I have a weekend pass."

"I go in early for the Wedgwoods' breakfast, and my day ends around 5:30 after tea."

"How about you tell me where I can meet you, and we'll have an early dinner? I know you'll be too tired for more than that after working a long day. Then I can get you home, and I'll get back to the base."

"That is a wery considerate offer," she said, and gave him detailed directions as to where they could meet. She was planning to be on time.

29

THE MORNING AFTER MEETING BERNARD

ositha awoke early in order to reach her employers' home in time to properly serve their breakfast. She did not have to prepare it, only to be certain that they received it in the correct bowls and dishes, with the appropriate cutlery and serviettes. Such fancy words, Rositha thought, for serving food while others were starving. Still, the family was good to her and would have provided her with anything which she needed.

She noticed how improved her mood seemed that morning. She was actually smiling with no one else around to see her. It could not have been the little wine which she had consumed the night before, as she had purposely had only a small quantity of alcohol to prove to herself that she was not destined to imbibe vast quantities of plum wine like her father and grandfather apparently had done. She suspected the smile arose from the prospect of seeing young Bernard again. "Well, no matter," she joked to herself, "he looks older with that thin hair, and who knows if he will actually show up this evening."

When she arrived at the Wedgwood Estate, her co-workers commented on her steps "seeming lighter" that day, but she pretended not to hear them. Then at 5:30 P.M. sharp, she was changed from her uniform into her street clothing, and was out the servants' entrance and around to the front gate. And there, true to character, stood Bernard in uniform with his cap in his hands. He, too, was grinning with pleasure as he took her arm and headed out toward the business district where they were certain to find a place for an early meal.

He seemed to be well able to afford the high prices which food now cost in the city, even though the meals were not fancy. They ate well, and, as they left, he handed her a chocolate bar. "GIs are always expected to carry these," he joked. "So I thought I'd prove my authenticity by bringing you one."

Rositha laughed and began eating it but did have the good graces to offer him a piece. His reply convinced her that she might be getting a kiss at the door, for he said, "I was thinking of sampling it as a secondhand treat."

And, after their bus ride, and a brief walk, they were at the side door to her apartment building. He asked, "May a GI kiss a Slovenian girl goodnight?"

She leaned forward, and their lips met for several seconds, before they both seemed a little embarrassed, and pulled apart. "I'll need to find out when you will let me try that again?" he said. And so, they parted with a date made for the end of that same week when their schedules would permit them the time.

Initially, Rositha thought it best to keep this as her own business, but Vilma had been aware of the blind date. While answering Vilma's questions about Bernard, she did say that they planned to keep seeing one another. This kind of commitment was unusual for

Rositha. She had the custom of weeding men out very quickly. That is, one small flaw, and they were sent packing; she could not tolerate poor manners, people who put other groups down, and men who denigrated women. Vilma wondered if this fellow really was so special, or if Rositha was simply getting less fussy as the war rolled on. In any case, Vilma did not have long to wait for an answer. It was now the Spring of 1944, and within two weeks Bernard announced to Rositha that he could not visit her for a little while because of a major mission to which the U.S. Army flyers were connected. She should not be worried as he would be safe, but very busy, and she would be on his mind the entire time. When he returned, and he promised that he would, he had an important question to ask of her.

Like any woman who was newly in love, Rositha's first question was "Is this legitimate? Does he have a special mission, or is he moving on?" Then she felt fear for him. "What terrible challenges are the military facing? Will he be safe?" Finally, she resigned herself to accepting his description of what was happening, as she could not learn more, but such mysteries were typical during war. He said he would think about her, and so she must agree to wait.

An odd question began to plague her. Perhaps it was born out of a need to buffer her desire for him when he was totally unavailable, but the truth was she did not know if she wanted to leave Europe to live in the USA for the rest of her life. Certainly, he would not wish to stay in London, or move back to Slovenia with her. Did she want to live in the quiet mountains of Vermont and recreate the life she had been so anxious to escape in Yugoslavia? Would this be the opportunity for which she had waited so long? And what about seeing her poor father and her siblings, God willing they should survive this war? It seemed she would be giving up a great deal for this man his fellow soldiers called "Red" due to his hair color. Is this what she wanted, Red and then ten little redheaded children?

Many days went by with no communication between them. Vilma said she had heard from her friends that most of the soldiers were acting in this way. Rositha should understand that it could not be helped. She grew restless, this much secrecy must be something major; and then it happened: The Invasion of Normandy. On June 6, 1944, the Allied Forces of land, sea and air banded together for the largest invasion in human history. It took place on the French shore of Normandy. They landed and kept on coming until, by the end of June, troops, supplies and vehicles had overwhelmed the area and the future of the war had turned around. Loss of life to the Allies was over 10,000 men, but for this effort the Germans would sign an unconditional surrender and end the war in May 1945. After the Invasion at Normandy, the Germans continued to fight, but this "D-Day" activity was regarded as the beginning of the end of the war.

However, news in the papers about that first day of fighting, June 6, could not predict the eventual outcome, but did announce the thousands of dead on both sides. The casualties sounded staggering. Those citizens of Europe reading this news, including Rositha, were terrified for the wellbeing of those whom they loved. It would be days before Bernard could contact Rositha, as telephone and telegraph wires were destroyed across large swatches of land. Bodies were being recovered from everywhere, and many missions were run simply to retrieve the wounded and dead; their rescue and treatment came first with everyone focused toward this goal.

When Rositha finally heard Bernard's voice again, it was through a ham radio operator who often intervened in these situations. She was asked to come to this fellow's house for an important message.

When her connection was made, and she recognized Bernard's voice, she broke down in sobs of joy. Her reaction was not lost on him.

Upon his return, Bernard proposed to her as soon as he was free to leave the base. He had found a small diamond ring which he could purchase with just a few borrowed pounds of extra help from his buddies, and the sale of one of the motorcycles that they had fixed-up. She was not concerned with the size of a stone but only cared that he was truly committed to her. Yes, he said he was sure of this decision, had written to his mother, and that she had said Rositha would be welcome to their Vermont home. His commanding officer gave his approval and, just as the war ended, they were married in one of the few Roman Catholic Churches in London.

This allowed them more time to get to know each other. It also gave Rositha more time to prepare Vilma for being left behind. Vilma had only existed, without at least one of her sisters when she was on that ship, so she hated the idea of separation. But as the war was coming to an end, it was a very jubilant yet confusing time. So many people were displaced, lost or missing that there was confusion and heartbreak everywhere. Vilma decided to be supportive of Rositha.

Rositha and Vilma had to find what each of them would need for their own transition, but they were also searching for word of their siblings and father. Most communication lines were down. The Red Cross was overwhelmed with requests, and people all over Europe begged for help with reunification. Families would discover that one member had made it to the USA, another to Australia, and a third was living in Canada. And they were the fortunate groups as so many would be gone without explanation.

30

SURVIVING DEFEAT
AND DISGRACE

Julijana had never anticipated that Adolf Hitler could win this war. She was too horrified by his goals and philosophy to think that the world would allow him to triumph. "That would have been evil overcoming good, and God would not permit this to last," she said to herself.

Believing this, still did not make being on the wrong side of this victory easy for those who had to capitulate. Hansi was humiliated, as were his so-called friends. Now none of them wished to admit their roles in the war or their connections to the Reich. They were also afraid of each other. If a "friend" knew of your activities, then that friend could turn you in to the Allies. Committees were popping up all over Germany seeking to identify those responsible for the massacres of the Jews which would come to be referred to as The Holocaust. If you had worked in a concentration camp, unless you were the lowest of laborers, such as kitchen staff, you were now considered a war criminal. Certainly, guards were among the most hated, right next to those who ordered hideous experiments on the

Jewish prisoners. These people had inflicted pain simply to satisfy their curiosity regarding different abuses the human body could endure.

There were many sick people who, once having conceived of some sadistic plan, would remain determined to carry it out, no matter that it offered no socially redeeming value. They would do multiple surgeries on young healthy legs to see if the human body could recover from some unnecessary procedure. And they might try to see if one person could do well without pain medication, and another without antiseptic drugs. This was why these horrible doctors were happy when twins showed up at the camps. They felt they could conduct better controlled studies if the subjects were identical. A difference in results could be attributed to the procedures used, rather than to a difference in subjects.

Some of these mad scientists made souvenirs out of their subjects' body parts once those subjects had passed away. They used human skin for making wallets and lampshades. These objects simply revealed the deeper level of depravity these "scientists" possessed and their pride at creating horror. There were drawers filled with such things when these men had to flee their laboratories. They were among the most despised for needlessly risking human life, but the guards who intentionally took lives were never forgiven either.

Such were the people fleeing Germany, or their original identities, just as fast as they could conjure up an escape route or an identity change. The more clever ones had long anticipated the possibility that a new persona would be required. They had passports with fake pictures, and tickets for South America, in strongboxes waiting for use. They were using any form of transportation which they could find to simply escape. Friendships were forgotten, a thing of the past, so Hansi could turn to none of his pack of friends.

But, this would work to their advantage; there was no one around to speak against them or to identify Hansi as a go-between. He was simply an artist whose work had been commissioned by those wishing to show themselves off in a flattering light. His job was to paint favorable portraits; he had no say as to how these works would be used. He did not know who belonged, or did not belong, to the Nazi party. He only knew what they wanted, and that he would be paid for his work. How else was he to provide food for his wife and son? He had been moved to this apartment, by those who needed his work since they were clustered, for some unknown reason, in this area. He accepted the apartment as it was in a relatively safe zone and provided easy access for his clients. He was an artist, and as such, knew nothing about politics.

Hansi and Julijana spoke about what they must do. They both thought it would be wise to get back to Vienna and reestablish themselves in their old neighborhood. They soon learned that, unfortunately, most of that area had been destroyed by bombs, but a renaissance was hoped for. Many people from the old area wanted to rebuild, start apartment buildings, cafés, and art shops where the old ones had been. The Danube was still there as an anchor, as were many opera houses, and cathedrals. It was a chance to rebuild. This became their plan, and Hansi would go along with their decision.

Haunting Julijana almost as much as how she, Peter, and Hansi would be safe, was her total lack of information regarding her siblings and her father. How had they managed to get through the war? She felt certain that Mojca and Vid had sailed to Australia, but then what had happened? They must have settled in, perhaps had a family, and she could easily imagine that they remained safe, but where were they?

But larger, more frightening questions loomed. She knew her darling little sisters, Rositha and Vilma, were in London. What had become of them? Had they escaped the bombing? How had they supported themselves? Were they able to get out of London if they needed to?

And finally, most frightening of all, the last thing she knew was that Andrej was not only married but in the Kings' Royal Army. How had he fared in this war? Back when they hid on the pletna to surprise thieving gangs, he had been anxious to use a gun and to demonstrate that he was in charge. Had he finally used a gun for real? How had that been for him? Was he safe and with his family or, lost on some lonely hillside after the kingdom came apart? Did he perish fighting for his king?

So Julijana was anxious for her own little family but also desperate to make contact with someone about her family of origin. She did not even know if her father was alive, and if so, who was helping him throughout all this rationing and terror. She prayed someone in the family was by his side.

And now she heard that the Russians would be in charge of Slovenia. Her father hated the Communists almost with the same ferocity with which he hated the Nazis. She hoped he would be wise and political enough to keep some of his opinions to himself. It was not necessary to tell new leaders that they had no business running "his" Slovenia. He could manage if he were careful. If not, she hoped that the Reds would at least be sympathetic to the attitudes of an elderly farmer, for he was unlikely to strike anyone.

Some of these thoughts almost made her smile. She wondered whom she might call, and then the priests popped into her mind. If they were still there, they would know the business of everyone in town: who had died, who had babies, who was married, and who was likely to need or provide help. She considered, for some time, trying to reach the Fathers, and then realized that learning much from them would raise for her many new issues. She was not ready to address either her son's paternity with these clerics, or to bring up the fact with Peter that Hansi was not his true father. These were very challenging times, especially as they felt both displaced and homeless, not an ideal time to add "Oh, by the way, son, the man you think is your father is really not."

She would put her son and husband first. They had survived the war, and they would find a home and then discover how her family had fared. She loved them all, and would pray for the best to be true.

31

THE GUARDS SEEM RESTLESS

Every prisoner becomes an expert in reading the body language of his guards. If they look miserable with baggy eyes and unshaved faces, then it never bodes well for the captives. There was a time when their captors had looked almost jovial with smiles, round bellies, and confident gestures as they forced the men through the paces of the morning on their way to a work detail. Now they were not letting them out of the camp to perform duties, there was almost no food to share, and the guards were as unkempt as the prisoners, although their clothing was not quite as ragged.

All the prisoners had all prayed for the victory of the Allied Forces, but as they watched the toll that losing was taking on their enemy, there was a certain fear added. What if they could not survive winning? What if the guards, in the pain of defeat, wished to annihilate these prisoners as token attacks on the victors whom they so despised? Would they now kill them just to feel a moment's revenge while their own world was so dark? Had the Yugoslavs suffered through years of humiliation and imprisonment only to perish as the war ended? What a cruel fate that would be.

The first night following these observations, which were neither confirmed nor denied by the guards as having any relevance, Andrej had vivid dreams. His thoughts appeared surrounded by barbed wire just as were his sleeping quarters. But then he was home on his family farm standing just outside the house and facing down the hill. Lake Bled was directly in front of him, and to his right was the ancient castle. The meadow grass had recently been cut, and birds were flying in and out of the flattened grass seeking bugs, and perhaps small snakes which would have been sliced through. These critters made easy eating. The freshly cut grass gave off a rich sweet floral smell of which Andrej could not get enough. In his dream he kept taking in deep breathes hoping to savor the scent for as long as possible.

The next thing he realized was that he was running down the hill, out of control, at a break-neck speed, and was headed for the lake. Fortunately, he had enough forethought to drop to his knees and then roll the last few yards right into the water. He was gasping for air and laughing. As he came up out of the water, he saw Rositha, a tiny child in his mind, rolling and laughing right into the water behind him. This gave him a rush of joy. They splashed each other for a time, and he remarked how cool and refreshing the lake felt, that they would not need baths that evening.

He also looked over toward the pletna, and one of them was out, probably carrying tourists. Maybe Mojca was selling her honey rolls. Oh, how he hoped there would be some leftovers to go with his breakfast. There was nothing sweeter than their family's honey and Mojca's cooking. Then he sank back into his slumber.

The next part of his dream had him in the woods with Ivan. They were stalking a deer, and he was both afraid of killing such a beautiful creature and excited to be a hero for the family when they were all so hungry. The woods were sparkling with dew at this moment; home had never seemed more picturesque, more idyllic. In this dream, his mother was still alive, and he felt a sense of her just standing a few feet away, wearing her apron, and awaiting their hunting triumph with a kettle bubbling filled with water to stew the organ meats. He would be sure to hug her for as long as he could just to be certain she knew how much he loved her.

Finally, his dreaming took him to his home in Serbia where his wife and baby Valerija continued their long wait for him. The baby was actually a little girl by now, and he wondered how long it would take her to recognize him, or to get to know him again. He was so pleased that this child was born; she was his hope for the future. No matter what happened she could keep him alive through her future children and his grandchildren. Where there were births, life would continue. He felt certain that his family had survived this horrible war and thanked God for their lives.

When he awoke from a nudge provided by his tent mate, it was with a sense of joy and love which these dreams had created. With these feelings in his heart, he received the tidings that the guards had snuck off in the night, and the camp was devoid of any German authority. They were not so much released as they were free to break out and find their way home. This word of freedom passed quickly among the men, then a huge cheer erupted and many of them, including Andrej, fell to their knees. Thanking God for being released from imprisonment after so long, and for being alive at the end of this bitter slice of history, seemed the least a good Catholic boy could offer.

The Red Cross was arriving in trucks as the men began stumbling over the barbed wire fences. They wanted to identify each prisoner as he left, and provide him with a change of clothing and a few rations to help sustain him on the long walk home. In many cases, the prisoners required medical attention which the Red Cross also provided. When they could offer transportation to the prisoner's home, they would do so, but most of the Yugoslavian men were going to travel along mountain passages to arrive home as expeditiously as possible. Trucks would not be capable of managing the terrain well, especially if there were other vehicles on the roads, and the spring snow melt had left them deep with mud.

Andrej registered his name and home address with the Red Cross, accepted fresh clothing and listened to their warning that the roads were dangerous because many soldiers were still fighting the war. He knew that the Partisans had always said "Join us or we will kill you." And he now understood that they were saying, "If you were not with us, we will kill you." Therefore, he thought it best to leave the remains of his Royal Army uniform behind and to dress like a simple farmer. As he changed his clothing, the only thing he found worthy of keeping was his "good luck toque," the red cap which he had picked up after the bombing in front of his sister's destroyed home in Vienna. He stuffed this under his shirt and into the belt of his pants.

But he, and most of the men who had been captives together, could not wait to get home, almost not believing that their own friends and neighbors would not receive them well. After the one phone call which The Red Cross was able to permit each man, and through which he learned that his wife and daughter were waiting for him, he set out on foot to leave Austria for Belgrade. Naturally, the first leg of this journey would take him home through Slovenia. Knowing that Marica was expecting him and would now be notifying the family of his release was high motivation for the trek ahead.

British soldiers appeared along the route to Yugoslavia, serving as guardians of the trail. They were assisting in directing traffic, as this was a time of massive confusion with all the rules changing and millions of displaced people seeking asylum or assistance in reaching distant locations. Much of the traffic mysteriously was flowing up the Ljubelj Pass, away from Yugoslavia. There were thousands of people, men, women, and children, with everything they owned tied to their backs and trying to get away from the Communists who now dominated their land. They wanted to get to Italy as they understood that, during the final days of the war, the Allies had split up responsibility for various factions of the Axis Union. Because of all the help the Partisans had provided to the Allies, they were rewarded with Russian oversight for most of Yugoslavia since the Partisans were Communists. The Americans had control of Italy, and the Yugoslavians believed they would be far better treated by the Americans than the Russians, so folks were attempting to walk to Italy. But, when they reached a certain point, the British were turning them back. It was a mistake on the part of these soldiers to think that the Reds would treat people well simply because they were countrymen and the war had ended. In most cases, the people who were turned back were also doomed.

Into this mix of confusion and suffering entered Andrej. He was buoyed by his euphoria at being free, and at having just made contact with his wife after four years of fear, doubt and loneliness. He would lend a hand when others were stuck in the mud, or pick up a pilgrim who had slipped and fallen, for freedom had helped his strength to flow again and his mind to clear. His fellow travelers were worried about returning to their homes. They spoke of Tito leading the Partisans throughout the war and now having big ideas.

No one could own anything to set him apart from his neighbors; there could be no titles, no wealth, and no superiority. Communism made them all equals, and they could be called upon to share their food and land. They understood that their sheep belonged to the country, not to themselves and that they would be required to give up God and never bow down to blessed Jesus.

Andrej told them all these matters would require time to resolve. He thought much of what they heard was hysteria due to the years of deprivation and uncertainty. He believed that all would be fine, but in the beginning, of course, there would be growing pains. And on he walked, as fast as he could manage, dying to be on Yugoslavian soil again.

32

THE QUEEN MARY

When the war ended, everything happened as though a motion picture were playing in fast forward. There was so much to do, and so much communication was finally opened up, that Rositha felt as though she was dizzy all the time. One of the first things that happened was that the U.S. Army wanted Bernard, and most of the troops, back in the United States. Bernard was shipped home on a "Liberty" ship even though he was attached to the Army Air Corps.

He seemed happy enough to go home once he had made sure that Rositha would follow and that the Army would watch out for her. She would be sailing on The Queen Mary which had not been accommodating passengers for several years. Just the ship's name amused Rositha to think of how she came to London and what a different course her life was now taking. She had to pack a small trunk, and everything she had ever wanted to take forward in her life would need to be in that container. Certainly, she could buy or make new things in America, but as far as anything sentimental or personal was concerned, she must select carefully. She made most of her decisions with regard to what would be needed on board the ship, and Bernard had said they could get anything else she needed in the Vermont General Store. Still, she had a good pair of snow boots she made certain to take along.

There were other challenging matters for her besides the paperwork necessary to prove she was an American's wife. One was parting with Vilma, who would now, be living without a sister in the next bed. They had graduated from the boarding house for respectable ladies, to a tiny apartment of their own with a shared bath in the hall. It was not luxurious, but it was better than living with a large group of women who were not always respectful of each other's space or property. They moved out when one too many of their pretty scarves had shown up on someone else at dinner; apparently, big city girls knew how to pick locks.

So it was Vilma's intention to stay in the apartment alone, or perhaps try to get a friend in as a roommate. It was just as well that Rositha couldn't take much in her trunk, as it might have left Vilma without some necessities. But as the time grew closer for Rositha's departure, they were increasingly anxious and often sharp with each other. This was mitigated in the very last week of Rositha's stay when Vilma became excited about a man she had just met. This certainly removed Rositha's guilt in leaving her sister, if she could think of her happily with a boyfriend.

The other problem seemed as though it would not so easily be resolved. Toward the end of May, when Rositha had called home again to see if her father and brother in Slovenia had been contacted by everyone in the family since the war ended, she got disturbing news. There was only one person unaccounted for, and that was her brother Andrej. He had been in touch with his wife, Marica, in Belgrade through the Red Cross. Following that call he had planned to reenter

Yugoslavia through the Ljubelj Pass according to his description of the next leg of trip he had mapped out. But since that time, when he sounded so near to home, there had been no word of him, none at all.

Her sister-in-law, his wife, had been contacting the Red Cross every other day, but their answer was always the same, "We have nine million displaced people right now. We are sure he will turn up. He did register his name and your address with us. We are certain he is on his way." And so she would try not to despair, but some days were more difficult than others.

Rositha had finally sent Bernard a telegram asking if he could think of any avenue they might pursue in trying to find Andrej, and, as he was back in the States, he felt helpless to intervene. If Andrej had been married to an American, there might have been steps they could take, but as things were, the U.S. State Department was overwhelmed simply trying to find all missing Americans.

Finally, the day came when Rositha would board the Queen Mary which loomed large and luxurious at the harbor. The ship looked formal in black, gold and silver with multiple decks. There were restaurants and lounges positioned in several locations, and she held two thousand one hundred passengers with an additional eleven hundred crew members. While the first-class passengers had comfortable staterooms close to the major dining rooms, Rositha was in a smaller chamber below these, but it was better than what other passengers received who were in very crowded rooms. She was lucky, as being married to an American had afforded her some benefits.

The trip was smooth. In six days Rositha would set foot on Ellis Island, New York, USA. Here she must be processed, her papers examined, her health status reviewed, and then, after many long lines, she would be reunited with her husband.

She recognized Bernard when he doffed his cap, and there was his beautiful, although thinning, red hair. They rushed to each other, and he planted a long kiss on her lips. When he pulled away, they were both blushing and giggling, as neither was accustomed to public displays of affection, nor did either of them feel entirely comfortable with the other after several months apart and so short a time married. But the real joy was in this moment actually materializing. They remembered all the long months of planning, the madness at the end of the war, and then the great distance to overcome to meet in a city with which neither of them was really acquainted.

The Vermont son could not wait to get his bride in his home. While some men would have booked a suite in the city for a second honeymoon, Bernard had booked a room in a hotel right next to the train depot back in Vermont. Then, when morning arrived, he would buy them breakfast and take her home to his mother.

Mother, Grace Adams, looked very much like Bernard would have if he gained fifty pounds and wore a housedress. While he was a nice looking man, the same could have been said of her. Still, her daughter-in-law was grateful to be joining them, and several pleasant days were passed while they attempted to acquaint her with their home and the area.

Rositha loved the bridges which tied Vermont to New Hampshire over the Connecticut River. And the area was, indeed, mountainous in a manner similar to her native Slovenia. The people she met were welcoming to her, with many wishing to give her gifts such as Vermont maple syrup and handmade mittens. She took everything with a pleasant "thank you."

But, after a few days, another message was conveyed by Grace, who was the Post Mistress of Fairlee, Vermont. She had thought

Bernard had made a good arrangement when he married Rositha and wanted her to join them in Vermont as both she and he would be working, and Rositha could be their housekeeper, having meals waiting on the table for them in the evenings.

While Rositha had been honored to work for Lord and Lady Wedgwood in a similar capacity, this was not her idea of starting off a marriage with her own home and with her own family. It did not take long for the new bridegroom to get the message. Within a month they had a small, third story walk-up apartment not far from the railroad tracks, but it was theirs.

Bernard's first job upon returning from the war was in the First National Stores who were competitors to A and P stores. It was not a high paying job, but his mechanical abilities and management style soon moved him into management in one of their branches, and made paying the bills much easier. When all the soldiers came home from the war, there was a business boom in the States, but also a pressure to reward these people who had served their country by seeing that they received adequate employment; not always easy to achieve.

Rositha had never expected the roads to be paved in gold. Vermont was very quiet, but she preferred quiet to the Blitz. Bernard had a brother whose wife and young daughter became good friends and good company for her. She was able to plant a few flowers on the edge of their parking space at the apartment house, and before 1946 was over, she was pregnant with their first child.

33

VILMA MUST GET ON
WITH HER LIFE

Vilma returned from work to an empty apartment on the day that Rositha had begun her travel to Southampton, and then on to the Queen Mary, headed for the USA. If she could have afforded to take time off, she would have liked to accompany her sister, but now that she must cover the rent with one paycheck, any time off was a grand luxury. Still, it might have helped to abate the shock of looking around her and seeing a half cleared closet and extra space on the dresser. A few photographs were also missing, and there was hollowness to the rooms which she had never noticed before, even when home alone for a few hours. She felt goose bumps on her back and gave a little shudder. "How do people stand it," she wondered living by oneself seemed so odd.

Then, to cheer herself up, she turned her thoughts to Samuel. They had only just begun seeing each other, but already she could tell this was different. He was a real English gentleman with a home in the country which sounded lovely and historic. He was considerate of her and very complimentary. He liked her accent saying it made her sound sexy. And, in reality, she was a petite blond with almost a kewpie doll face. Around Samuel she was always smiling, as the loneliness went away, and he gave her hope for the future. She had started to feel terrified that she would never find a husband, as the war had taken so many men away, but here he was, eligible and attractive.

Now, with her sister married and gone, Vilma felt it was definitely her time for a serious romance of her own. She just wished she had Rositha's mature judgment to help her decide how she should handle situations which were bound to arise. It seemed that the wind rattled in the old chimney too much this evening, and her soup didn't heat so well as when her sister prepared it for her. "Oh, dear," she sighed, "I'd better get on with my life."

The next evening Samuel had said he would stop around to see how she was doing on her own. He brought a bouquet of flowers, which were finally again available from vendors on the street corners, and a bottle of wine. She laughed saying "The perfect year to accompany goulash," for that was what she had the ingredients to make. She had rather hoped he would be taking her to a pub for fish and chips but the flowers and wine signaled that she must be cooking. This actually provided Samuel more time to romance Vilma.

As she was browning the onions and meat, he came up behind her and began by kissing her neck which was quite exposed due to the position she was bent in over the stove top. It was a pleasant feeling and made her knees feel weak. Still, she was determined to remain a virgin until married, although certain other sexual adventures were not out of the question; and she definitely craved the attention. This felt like a dilemma which he seemed pleased to stimulate. Once that bottle of wine was consumed she realized they were both on the brink of not turning back when suddenly there was a commotion in the hallway as two other tenants seemed to be fighting over who was first in queue for the loo. Shakily Vilma rose to her feet and said, "It is really getting late, perhaps another time?" And she smiled.

Samuel looked frustrated, but it had the effect which nothing else previously had brought out in him, an invitation to go with him that weekend to his family estate. She said she thought she could clear her calendar. And when he left, she felt as though she had just won some sort of prize. Still, she heard Rositha's warning sounding in her head, "Who will buy a cow if milk is free?" And she wondered what it would take to remain chaste if she was sleeping overnight at his family home? "We shall see" was all she thought.

That Friday seemed to take forever to arrive, as though it were a week of nights waiting for the Blitz to be over and the all-clear signal to sound because Vilma was so excited to meet his family and see his home. She believed this weekend would be pivotal to their future. He came by the apartment building promptly at 4:30PM and was driving an old Bentley. He came up the stairs for her and took her bag. He seemed solicitous and very genteel. Those simple gestures made a positive impression on the anxious woman who used them as signs that she should relax and be happy.

The conversation along the forty-five-minute drive was at first awkward and then rather good natured fun. He joked once as to what she had brought for his dinner, but then he quickly put her at ease that it was a joke. "My parents have a small staff to take care of that sort of thing," he finally said. "And on Fridays they often insist on fish or chicken unless my father has shot something." When he saw her shocked and perplexed expression, he hastily added, "Like quail or pheasant."

"That sounds delicious," she said.

But when they arrived, Samuel appeared a bit dismayed that his parents were, indeed, at home for the weekend. He had actually thought they had a commitment at the sea and could barely contain his disappointment that they were at home. Furthermore, his parents were surprised that he had a guest with him, which he tried to pretend was them being forgetful. It was a most awkward introduction but one which they graciously covered over by welcoming Vilma good naturedly and insisting that her arrival would make it a lovely weekend.

And lovely it was. The estate consisted of a large manor house built of brick with a shared central area and then wings for the owners and guests, and a separate area for the help. The kitchen took up nearly the entire basement area with copper pans and kettles hanging on the walls and on cooking hooks over the fire, and several large bake ovens. The house was easily several hundred years old but the kitchen had clearly been remodeled recently to make use of gas and electric appliances. There was also a wine cellar just below one half of the kitchen.

The dining room had a long table in front of a roaring fire, and the walls were adorned with several of the trophies Samuel's father had taken over the years. All the rooms were large but not as massive as might be found in a castle. Additionally, they were all well-lit and quite warm by contrast with a stone castle. Homey and cheerful was the effect it had on Vilma. Handmade quilts and real wool sweaters were also part of the decor. In some ways, it reminded her of Slovenia if Slovenia could ever have prospered and grown without a war creeping into its economic situation every decade or so.

Samuel's parents were creative and engaging. They endeavored to draw Vilma into conversation and asked about the length of her relationship with Samuel. Vilma turned to him to allow him the privilege of responding to the question, but he only stammered a little and might actually have been apologizing for her presence once again. She let this go as to do otherwise would have signaled disaster; still he seemed less genuine than she had originally thought. But as soon as they were alone he apologized saying it was always agony for him to try and respond to his parents' inquisitions and couldn't he compensate her with a kiss? Then they had a sweet groping session before dressing for dinner.

After dinner, his parents retired early and bid them to have a lovely evening. Samuel took Vilma for a little walk out to the barns and showed her their horses which she dutifully admired. Then, while they seemed finally in a very private setting, he set upon her with great zeal telling her how beautiful she was and how badly he desired her. They were moving very quickly and had gone from leaning on an inside stall to falling into a bed of hay with no sense of time, place, or restraint. He had his full weight on her, and Vilma was both loving it and becoming frightened that she was about to go too far, when the groomsman came in, as he did not know why there were lights on.

When he saw Samuel, he called him "Sir" and began to back out of the barn apologizing. But, perhaps to save face as it seemed as though they could have had a bedroom, Samuel jumped up and helped Vilma up too, with a great deal of levity, so that they were both laughing about the situation. Finally, they said good-night to the groomsman and left for the house.

There were several other buildings on the property, some with thatched roofs, but this night they went back into the house. Samuel did seem rather out of sorts, so they kissed very lightly and went to their separate rooms. It was the first moment Vilma had felt a chill in that lovely house. Of course, the next day they ended up going to a fair with his parents and the big romantic adventure for which Samuel had craved, disappeared for the time being.

34

THE DRIVE BACK TO LONDON

On Sunday afternoon, Samuel, still acting gracious in front of his parents, indicated to Vilma that it was time to pack her things so that he could drive her back to London. She heartily thanked his parents and stated again what a beautiful home they had, and how pleased she was to have met them. She departed hoping that there would be more times like this and that she had left a favorable impression.

When they were sequestered in the automobile, Samuel said, "You didn't have to overdo it with my parents. They knew you had enjoyed yourself and their company."

"I see," Vilma said, "vell I was raised to be certain people were thanked for extending a kindness and that it is better to over-thank than to under-thank."

"If that's even a word," he grumbled. "Well, you did that right then."

Although his words sounded accepting enough, she could not deny the undercurrent of sarcasm to the remark, but, once again, thought it was better to let it go than to bring on a possible argument.

Instead she said, "And I am most grateful to you, Samuel. It was a lovely veekend."

Following this exchange, he was barely communicative, and she decided to simply relax on the trip home. He did remark, at one juncture, as to the cost of petrol and the sum of coupons he was expending to give her a ride. "Had I known," said Vilma, "I could have sought a train seat and perhaps have been met at the station."

"No, of course not," he added. "You are worth the trouble and expense; I was a bore to even mention it." Then he hastily added, "But, if you like, I can spend the night and that will compensate me."

Vilma didn't like the sound of this. She replied, "If you are too tired to drive you may certainly use my couch but I must be able to vork in the morning." He made no response.

When they got to her apartment, he pulled her bag out of the boot and handed it to her at the curb. He said, "I trust you can carry this for the rest of the way. I had better make a hasty trip home, as my father expects a little help on the property in the morning." No further explanation was given.

Although hurt by his curtness, she said only, "Very vell. Thank you again and have a safe journey."

Then, she somewhat shakily made her way into the apartment lobby. Her thoughts were mixed. Had she insulted Samuel by protecting her virtue too intently; was he so fragile in character that he could not withstand a bit of a disappointment, even though she had made him no promises; or was something else out of order? Confused and anxious she made her way upstairs, and after a brief cry, ambled into bed when she realized that there had been no mention of a "next time." Could she have come across as cold and had she actually hurt his feelings? Then she fell asleep remembering that Rositha had said that men wish to pursue, she should have worried more if she had given him too much. With that, Vilma sighed and fell asleep; the sleep would put her confused mind to rest.

In the morning, Vilma busied herself with washing, watering her plants, packing her lunch and rushing to work along with most of London. It wasn't until she got to work, and friends asked how her weekend had gone, that she began to wonder how this could be answered. Yes, it had been a lovely weekend, and no, he had seemed cool and detached because she wouldn't "come across"? Was that the honest reply to their inquiries? She'd just have to give it time.

She didn't hear from Samuel that first night after work but reasoned that he had much to do for his family. When the second night passed without hearing her name called from the lobby to come for a telephone call, she actually inquired if there had been any calls for her that perhaps she could have missed. But the answer was a disappointing, "No, sorry love."

The next night, she did not wish to humiliate herself further by asking again about a call, so she just made certain that she was within ear-shot of the lobby. Finally, it was Friday night, and some of the girls asked if she'd like to go to the dance with them that evening. She started to say "No, thank you" so that she could wait by the telephone, but then thought better of it. What if she waited all night and he never called? She could hear Rositha saying, "Go out and have fun. If he tries to reach you and cannot, it serves him right."

Vilma danced, drank, and laughed all evening. Her friends remarked as to how gay she seemed and she simply reinforced her act by saying it was a fun night. But, all the time, nagging at her heart, was the thought that she prayed there would be a message from Samuel waiting for her. But, there was not a message; not that night, nor any night the following week. As she turned off the light each evening while getting into bed, she would tell herself not to despair. If he was gone so easily then he was no more suited for her than a squirrel was for a duckling. She must have felt the wrong signals. But after so saying to herself, she would then end up praying and begging God for just one more chance with him. Towards the very end of that second week, he appeared on her doorstep shortly before she was to meet up with the girls for another local dance.

"Looks like you are going somewhere?" he said glibly.

"Why yes, I am," was Vilma's reply. "A girl has to have some fun."

"Well," said Samuel, "I thought you were my steady, meeting my parents as you have."

"Indeed? Perhaps I don't yet understand the meaning of that English vord 'steady'," she retorted.

"I've been gone too long, have I," replied Samuel?

"Only if you intend on us being serious, but you are a fine, friwolous beau," she replied. Naturally she pronounced the word frivolous with a "w" instead of the "v." He was quick to mock her but seemed to be doing it with a good nature. Then they both laughed a bit, and he asked if he could take her to dinner.

In truth, she was so happy to see him, and thought that her prayers had been answered, that she accepted the dinner date. They had a lovely plate of fish and chips each with a beer. Then they went back to her flat and she invited him in "so long as you are a gentleman." He was a gentleman for about thirty minutes and then he began to tell her again how beautiful she was and how much he wanted her. "Forever?" she asked as he knew her fear of being used by a man.

"I do want you forever," he said. "We have already done many things with each other, wonderful, pleasurable things. Was there any harm in them?"

"No harm," she replied, "but my church requires that I have the sacrament of marriage before I do any more than we have done."

"You mean God cares if I caress you two inches lower or deeper than I have done already?"

She said, "Don't be cheeky. I cannot get pregnant from your kisses no matter where they fall, but if you use your penis, then I am in trouble."

That night, despite this conversation, and Vilma's pointed remarks, Samuel was relentlessly in pursuit of his goal. He even went so far as to say that he loved her. The use of this word, and the terror she had felt when she thought that she had lost him, led to an action that finally left him satisfied.

35

HAPPY YEARS AND YEARS OF DISMAY

Naturally, the first weeks after Samuel had started making love to Vilma in full were, for her, a time of complex feelings. She did enjoy the experience of sex, but her Catholic upbringing made it a time of constant sorrow. She was always making excuses to God for why she was weak, and going to confession to try to be absolved of her sins. The biggest problem was that she never truly intended to stop the behavior; at best, she only hoped to decrease it, or substitute something which the Priest might forgive, and yet, would be substantial enough to satisfy Samuel. Once they were in each other's arms there never appeared to be any going back to the days prior to their going all the way. Vilma loved being loved, and did not know how to keep from slipping into their established pattern.

After several months, with Vilma always anxious until her next menses had started, Samuel proposed that they begin looking for a better home. He wanted more privacy which a townhouse could provide. Typically, a townhouse was three floors of rooms on top of each other. That way they could have a private bathroom and even rent out a room or two to help with expenses. He wasn't pledging to live with Vilma fulltime, as he still had responsibilities with his parents, he declared, but he would help with the costs. And this added commitment of contributing monetarily for the rent, gave her more faith in him; in them. So it had the desired effect of making her less anxious but also a little less diligent of guarding her body.

She still insisted that he purchase condoms, which were a mortal sin for a Catholic to use, but in London, a Protestant city, and in areas which soldiers had frequented, there was always a way to get some, even if through the black market. She said that she would rather feel like a criminal than to have proof of her bedroom activities shown in public with a bonnet on. He laughed, but took every opportunity he could to enjoy complete freedom with "his woman." Of course, it was not too many months before her period was late and then failed to show up.

Vilma was frantic throughout those two weeks before they became certain that she was pregnant. Every chance she had to run into a loo and check to see if there was any sign of menstrual blood, she would take it. Her co-workers noticed her frequent trips down the hall and asked her if she was well. Naturally, she denied any problem. It was much too soon to tell anyone, and maybe "it" would go away. She would deal with what to say when she knew that she must.

Samuel, for his part, was also anxious, but not filled with the handwringing anxiety expressed constantly by Vilma. Still, he said, "We might as well have all the sex we can if there is no issue now with conception."

When this made her angry, he added, "I'm just trying to make the most of a bad thing. You know I love you."

And so, she comforted herself with the thought that he must love her, as he had not taken off the moment this change had apparently occurred. Still, when she was able to get the results in hand a few weeks later by seeing a doctor and finding out that, yes, she was indeed pregnant, he did not appear overjoyed. He even suggested that there were people he could find that would take care of this sort of thing and that he would handle the expenses, of course. But, Vilma was a good Catholic girl, and she loved the idea of having a baby, maybe even his baby, so that avenue was simply a dead-end. She told him she did not want to hear anything more about it. And again, he was able to sooth her and stay in her good graces, but there was no offer of marriage.

Dutifully, Vilma continued about her life as though nothing significant was about to erupt; as though her middle would not soon explode making her very personal life public. "Oh, you're pregnant, when are you due? I didn't even know you and Samuel were married. Do you want a girl or a boy?" All these things were said to her without any apparent hesitation. Didn't those who queried know that she was dying of mortification? But, on it went, typical responses to an atypical circumstance, or so she thought.

Finally, Vilma wrote to Rositha, who was quick to respond and guardedly positive about Vilma's baby. It seemed that both women were scheduled to give birth in late August, 1947. Rositha understood that Samuel had not yet proposed marriage, although Rositha thought that he would as soon as he got used to the idea, or as soon as his parents took interest in being grandparents, or as soon as they met the baby. Every few weeks Vilma prayed that the necessary stage had been reached for him to step-up and be a responsible parent. Nothing appeared to bring this out in Samuel, but he was there to drive Vilma to the hospital and to help carry in the necessary food and nappies.

The next two years went by fairly happily. Vilma had a beautiful baby girl one week after Rositha had a rugged baby boy. The sisters enjoyed their long distance comparison of notes on the children. Rositha never asked about Samuel's intentions, and Vilma made no remarks on the matter. There were a smattering of actresses having babies out of wedlock at this time, and Vilma told herself she was avant-garde. But inside, she longed for Samuel to make things right. She wasn't really certain if his parents even knew that they were grandparents. Samuel would mention their "good wishes," but they strangely never asked to meet the baby.

Near the time little Caroline was two years old, Samuel started staying away some nights. Initially he had seemed to want to be home with this beautiful baby, but other matters apparently demanded his attention. His behavior began to irritate Vilma; she thought that she had already sacrificed enough for this relationship. She asked Samuel to pick the baby up from the nanny and get dinner started, as she always returned home later in the afternoon than was ideal. He complied for two or three days and then informed Vilma that things were really not working out for him.

"Are you saying, "She asked, "that being a parent is a good deal of vork and you vant to have more fun?"

"Well," said Samuel, "I wouldn't put it like that, but I don't think you and I are going to make it."

Vilma was crushed. All her fears were coming true. She was being abandoned with the responsibility of raising a baby alone in a war-ravaged city far from home. She was still going to church, but it did not feel the same, and now she would be an object of pity.

If he had not also lowered his financial commitment to them, as a family, she might have had some respect left for him, but he also wanted to save money on his daughter! She thought that she was as angry as ever she could be until one month later when his wedding was announced in the paper.

Vilma raged and wept, then went into a slump. She could barely eat or function. Somehow, for the baby's sake, she kept it together. Finally, she confided all in the priest who was a nice man from Slovenia. In his congregation he had quite a number of expatriates from Slovenia. They had frequent meetings and social events. They celebrated holidays together in the way of the old traditions. She felt more comfortable within herself, as many of them had been through so much more given the war years. Some were even afraid of going anywhere near Yugoslavia out of fear of being murdered for their roles, or those of family members, during the war; or perhaps for what they had witnessed.

After a few years, a very shy Slovenian man began to court the still pretty Vilma who had the sweetest little daughter. But Vilma was careful not to go too far with this fellow as he was a good Catholic, yet he did not condemn her regarding her past.

Two weeks before they were married, Vilma destroyed all images of Samuel in her photographs. She did not want any reminders of his betrayals. And she did not wish to offend the man who was so happy to marry her and help to raise their child.

36

WALKING FREEDOM'S TRAIL

There was mud and misery in front of Andrej at every turn. Thousands of people jammed the passages trying to get to Italy. As he endeavored to pass one way, they walked across his path in another direction. Many of the people walking toward Yugoslavia were warning these throngs that they would not be permitted through to Italy, that the British Army was turning them all back; that they "have to give Russian governance a chance" said the British soldiers.

"Don't you mean those murderous Red swine running through the woods attacking anyone they please?" was the gist of the replies these pilgrims would make. They were not going back to be robbed, abused and murdered. They planned to try and get through the British barricades. Sadly, they would have to give up and go back the way they had come but could not accept the advice along the corridor. This would also not bode well for their longevity.

Andrej was pleased to help direct folks to return home, as that was where he most wanted to be, and it had never occurred to him that he would one day wish to live in Italy. However, after many of the men who were heading in the direction opposite to Andrej also tried to offer him advice, he began to question his own thinking. What they were saying made Slovenia sound like a hunting ground for human beings. The Germans had been running through the woods trying to find and liquidate the Partisans. The surviving Royal Army, and a few calling themselves the Home Guard, was still fighting the Germans but with no sympathy for the Communist Partisans. The Catholic priests continued to speak ill of these Partisans, who saw themselves as the volunteer champions of their people. The Partisans remained loyal to a Communist doctrine which denied religion to its people. Many blamed this on Comrade Tito who was referred to as an Austrian Corporal running around telling the Partisans how best to save their country. If it sounds chaotic, it was. But Tito had made the Partisans a bit less chaotic by organizing them into regions and naming buildings which they could claim as headquarters. These forces then truly claimed to be working for the Allies, and the Partisans hated the Nazis, thus earning the reward of Yugoslavia being given to the Russians at the end of the war as their share from the other Allies.

Animosity had not given way simply because the Royal Army and some Guard members plus the Partisans had a common enemy in the Nazis, there were other forces fighting as well. If anything, the anger and hatred for all factions had expanded until it exploded like a rotting corpse in the heat of battle. The Partisans wanted to annihilate anyone associated with the organization of the Church and those who wished to own their own land and cattle separate from the community. The Partisans still lived in the woods and took what they wanted. They were their own court, judge and jury. They wanted to put a bullet in the backs of all those who had not fought directly with them. And they were deadly serious. For them the war was only partly finished. Tito did not want adversity in his new country. If those who opposed him planned to be vocal, then they were to be eliminated. The Partisans knew what he wanted and were obliging.

All over Yugoslavia names were appearing on lists posted in public places. These lists contained the names of those who were no longer a problem and those who might be gotten out of the way soon. Even if a name were not posted, an individual should hesitate before toasting the heavens, as names could be added at anytime, either before or after liquidation. Andrej did not know it, but his name appeared high on this list. It seems the Partisan men he had challenged prior to the coup regarding Peter II, and the attack of the Germans on the Kingdom of Yugoslavia, had remembered him as arrogant in his fancy uniform. They were determined to make a lesson of him for all to see.

One issue arose before Andrej even crossed back into Slovenia, as both he and his father bore the same name. The list did not distinguish between the first and the second, but there on the wall of the train station, was a sheet of paper listing Andrej Lovrenc.

Andrej senior was a man of seventy-seven-years of age. His wife had died, and most of his children were out of touch, dispersed he knew not where, all over the world, at least in his mind. He and his son, Ivan had made it through some lean years on the farm, while others fought and took their goods if they so chose. He had gone hungry many nights, and others he had trembled in the cold for a lack of firewood. As fast as he would split enough to keep even part of the house warm, the Partisans would harvest it for their own needs. But he heard that the war was over, and, even if some of the boys were still camping in the woods, he wished to get back to normal.

He hitched a cow up to his cart and planned to make a trip in close enough to Ljubljana to trade a deer hide for some supplies.

He even hoped there might be a sign posted earlier along the route offering cheese or sausage for trade. He just wanted a little simple food to help sustain them and saw no harm in a short ride.

But he had not gone far when a group of "thugs," as he called them, stopped him and demanded to know his business. Rather than raise trouble he told them that he was hungry and was going to see about getting some food. The woodsmen began to ridicule him. "Why should anyone give you food, old man?" they asked.

He replied that he would make a fair trade for anything he might acquire, and that is when they decided to look more closely into his wagon. Then they wanted to know how he had survived all this time and not eaten the cow. He explained that the cow wouldn't be very tender, but she still gave milk and he used her manure for fertilizer. Of course they had something funny and mean to say about that.

Just when it seemed that they were about to let the old man go one of them asked for his name. He gave it with pride, as he had always felt he was an important part of the community running the pletna as well as a farm and, in the past, a roofing business. A furrowed brow was shown and then another. Like old St. Nick, except they were the devils, they checked their list. Right near the top, in a place held for the worst offenders, was his name.

When they asked him to spell his name so that there could be no mistake, he did so. When he realized that they thought he was an enemy of the people, he did not shout out "Oh, but that's my son's name too," for he did not wish to pass any harm on to his son, whom he believed to be a war hero.

So with very little protest, he followed them to the next town where they made a call. He was ordered out of his wagon and into a bare room to which they had access. When they saw him struggling to walk, they looked at each other. Their eyes seemed to say "Could this really be the one we are looking for?" But they just left him in the room and appeared to go somewhere for lunch.

After about five minutes, Andrej Sr. decided the best move was to go home. He went back outside and found his cow and wagon just as he had left them around the corner from this building. He unhitched the creature from where she had been tied to a post, turned her around and they walked back toward home. After about thirty minutes Andrej thought it might be a good idea to get off the road in case anyone was looking for him, so he pulled into a barnyard where his wagon wouldn't be visible from the road.

Once the farmer came out, they realized that they knew each other. Although it wasn't a very trusting time in their country, old Andrej told the farmer enough about his story to get his deer hide traded for both sausage and cheese and an invitation to stay for soup. It seems this was a fairly productive farm and one which was in the ownership of hardworking Catholics.

For the rest of his life, Andrej would delight in telling most of this story as "the day he escaped from the Partisan firing squad." He never liked thinking about why his son's name was on that list, or what it might have meant for his son's future, but it was a good escape for an old rascal. And he and Ivan ate a better meal that night due to his efforts.

The woodsmen did go easy on the old man. They may not even have minded that he escaped, but this was the last time the Lovrenc family would ever have a good dealing with any of them.

37

THE JOY OF HOMECOMING

There were not many telephones yet in the village where Marica and Andrej had made their home. Generally, one phone every few miles would serve the area well. Family was told the name of the families who housed the phones, and everyone was careful not to call too often, and to always be polite. But if family "A" received a call for family "B" they were obliged to either run up to a half mile to get someone, or to take an elaborate message. During war times there was very little opportunity to establish an appointment for a call, which would have allowed the recipient to be waiting by the phone at their friend's home.

Most of the farms were not too far apart, as their land fanned out behind them, leaving the buildings closer together in a hub of the wheel formation. This made sharing of food, information, or the telephone more practical. In this way, Marica had heard her husband's voice for the first time in four years. A neighbor had come running to her side porch shouting: "It's The Red Cross with Andrej on the line! He wants to speak with his wife! Marica, come quickly! It's

Andrej!" And Marica understood the shouting and dashed to run back to the neighbors' house.

In just the few minutes he was allotted to speak, for hundreds of others were queued up behind him, he said the words she had dreamed of hearing. "Marica, it is me, Andrej, I am alive and well enough. Are you and Valerija well? I love you and miss you and am on my way home."

She had given a breathless, flustered, reply to his words also including that she loved him. She asked, "How will you get home?"

And his reply was, "I would fly if I could, but I am walking. Soon, Marica, soon, I must go now." And then he was gone. She stood there, staring at the phone, before she realized that the neighbor was waiting for her. She handed the phone back on its overly stretched cord, as she was coming out of her daze, and thanked the woman profusely. This neighbor seemed happy for her, and the joy of that moment launched Marica's spirits into the sky. Marica skipped all the way back to her kitchen.

Although Marica had been married nearly six years and had a beautiful little girl, she still felt like a bride. Her darling husband had stayed by their side for as long as he could, but, before the baby was one-and a half years-old, he had been captured by the Germans and taken somewhere, in Austria to work in a Nazi POW camp. She knew he was forced to serve the Reich by cleaning up after Allied bombings occurring around him. Therefore, he was at least kept near Vienna, for that was a prime target of the Americans. He had been able to send about three letters but not permitted to disclose his location or precise duties. From reading between the lines she knew he was in an area where he had once visited his oldest sister and from where he did not feel too far from his parents' homestead.

He joked that he would just have to walk a few hundred kilometers, and he'd be back with Ivan putting a deer in the barn to hang.

Marica could imagine this reminiscing was a comfort to Andrej in his loneliness as he missed them all. She could also tell from his stories, and from what she heard about conditions in the POW camps, that he was hungry, for he went on to reiterate the many meals his mother had eked out of that one deer from years ago. The tale began with the stews and ended with broth, shoes and soap. One thing Marica would be certain to have on hand would be plenty of food for this poor man, even if she had to steal a chicken out from under the "red-devil's feet" which was how she described the Communists among them.

Her duties right now felt so pleasant, with a focus on coming joy rather than on being surrounded by uncertainty, death and destruction. She needed to find a piece of fabric; perhaps a dress of her own or her mother's which was in good condition, from which she could cut out two yards of material to make a lovely dress for their daughter, Valerija, to wear for her father's homecoming. He had not seen her since she was eighteen months old and now she was a charming little girl. While making her dress, they practiced greetings she could recite to her father upon his return. Then Marica would make herself something pretty to wear but not to greet him in; no, this would be a night gown, and she thought not to wear it long, then she blushed and giggled and tried not to think too much about lovemaking, although she was, in her own mind, still that young bride.

She was also determined that Andrej should not return to an alarming number of household chores. She had the help of one of her brothers in keeping the roof from leaking, and it looked straight and solid. Whenever there had been a storm, she had gone around the edges of the roof with a hooked stick and made certain nothing was blocking the drains that could lead to an overflow or back-up. She had recently painted the front door, although she could not make up enough paint for the gate and side door. Still, she reasoned, he will look first at the front door and see that all is well.

On the days when it was not pleasant enough to work in the yard, she switched to indoor cleaning. The curtains were taken down and washed, then dried as soon as the sun shone again. She stitched new bedding from material given to them on the occasion of their wedding for there had not been time to make many things then, as the war was starting. And she washed the house interior so well that it truly lightened the color of the rooms. While all the curtains were being cleaned she swept her floors, washed them, and then beat the rugs before putting them back down. To some friends, this work sounded like drudgery, but, to Marica, it was pure joy. She was planning for Andrej's return, and she was so excited that she required this work to keep from spinning like a top and exploding up the chimney, so great was her excitement and joy!

Her one brother that had remained home from the war due to a breathing problem had visited frequently to help with the crops. He had tilled the soil leaving her to plant, cultivate and weed, but she had managed these things. With so much to worry about, and a little girl who was often tended to by Marica's own parents, she needed the vigorous exercise of the hoeing to keep her energy channeled in a positive direction.

There had been one afternoon when she was alone on the farm, and some Partisans had arrived demanding food and cash. She had told them that she would send them away with plenty of food, and some beer her brother had prepared, but she hadn't a bit of cash to her name. Then they started joking that they would settle for the food and a roll in the hay. She was frightened but decided not to bring up her husband who was a captive of the Germans. Although this bunch of louts hated the Nazis, they might also conclude that Andrej was in the King's Royal Guard and want to cause both her husband and her more pain, so she thought it better to say nothing about her man. And if they were curious, they failed to raise a question perhaps themselves not wanting to cause more trouble. In the end, she gave them a nice quilt along with the food, and they left without trouble, probably knowing the quilt would be much more pleasant than tangling with a woman who seemed to be maintaining this much property by herself. Marica also had a gun hidden in her bedroom just in case she had to defend her own honor or protect Valerija while Andrej was away.

But most of her days were pleasant and exciting; everything she did, she did with Andrej in mind, how he would like this or that, would he notice that she had woven a new carpet, would he see the new fence, or notice that she had managed to expand the number of chickens? The pent-up excitement and worry of the last four years was about to have an outlet. She could feel their home again filled with laughter and merriment and hear their daughter squealing with joy to dance around the house in her father's arms. The wait should not be much longer she told herself, she had made it this far, just a little more time and they would be reunited. She would go to Church again later that day. She had hoped her Orthodox Church here in Belgrade would work as well as the church, in which Andrej's family had always worshiped, and it seemed the Roman Catholic Church and the Orthodox Church had the same terrible enemies.

These crazy Partisans, who were so well thought of by the Allies, had better content themselves with the Allied victory over the Axis, but she feared them almost as much as the Nazis. The Nazis were horrible, demented, racially motivated, genetic manipulators who wanted to control the peoples of the world. Yet, the Communists were not much different. They would slaughter their own people for the sake of ideology and they also did not care about the lives of others when it came to protecting their party from interference by other forces; it was their way or the graveyard: A smaller population was fine with them as long as those who remained shared their ideology. Like the Nazis, they believed that great achievements would arise once they all thought alike and would, therefore, move as a collective force towards achievements for all.

Marica prayed that this would now be a time when Yugoslavian people, whether they were Serbian, Croatian, or Slovenian, would work together to rebuild this country so affected by the war and loss. And soon, Andrej would be home to work along beside her for the sake of their family and a peaceful nation.

38

THE ROUGH ROADS CONTINUE

Andrej wondered when he would be free of all these crowds. Initially, he had felt exuberant to see so many of his countrymen after years on foreign soil, but, after many miles of witnessing confusion and hearing terrible stories from his homeland, he just wanted to see for himself. He could not imagine that the beautiful hillsides, lakes and streams had lost their sparkle; had hunger caused all the deer to be depleted by hunters; and were there no longer cows to produce the milk, cream, and cheese he so loved? Were the churches destroyed? Certainly, the larger ones must remain giving shelter to the poor…or so thought Andrej, not being able to visualize how his country had changed while he lived in war-torn Austria. But, the masses he was seeing as they fled the Kingdom of Serbs, Croats, and Slovenes were no longer safe at home. They were giving up much, but they believed a better place was just over the hills in Italy, where they would not be ruled by the Communist forces.

He didn't know enough to be forewarned, or if he suspected that all was not right, the memory of his wife's dear voice would lead him to their little farm outside of Belgrade, even if he was told that it was crawling with dinosaurs. Marica and Valerija were waiting for him, and that was his sole destination, his obsession. But he was hoping for some pleasant hiking as he used to remember it; the beautiful walks in the hills of Slovenia where there were many rock formations and, around many corners, waterfalls, lakes, and vistas as from the top of a gorge. He would feel like the master of the universe to stand on a high rocky outcrop and see nature cascading below him. If the walk was going to take days, at least he hoped he could enjoy it and be at peace. But the thousands of refugees fleeing towards Italy were not to permit this; their wagons, cattle, and sometimes pets, kept him from having even a moment of solitude.

He had made some progress by walking around the quagmire others were stuck in, both literally and figuratively. He no longer tried to help each group along his route by freeing them from the mud, or by advising them to go back, as the British soldiers had been insisting. Now his goal was to avoid anything, or anybody, who might prevent his forward motion. The war was over and he was on his way home to Belgrade!

Finally, he observed an opening between some rocks. It appeared to be a footpath, and pine trees were its background in the distance. Andrej was quick to slip in between those rocks. It was little used undoubtedly, as the others were carrying burdensome packages, family, and/or, traveling by wagon. No man carrying a basket would make it through this path. How fortunate for Andrej that he bore only a backpack and was slender after years of POW food. Then he laughed to himself that his losses would now be an advantage.

He stepped around the trees and found the earth solid, no more mud, animal waste, and the debris of travelers dropping possessions to lighten their loads. He was following the pass but on a footpath which seemed private. He tried to keep his pace steady, as this open atmosphere tempted him to gallop as though on horseback; he was filled with joy, as though again a child. Then a terrible thought entered his mind. He recalled being on patrol near Belgrade shortly before the battle in which he was arrested. Everything had looked good and then, without warning, he and his men had been attacked. It was an error in judgment which had almost cost him his life and had resulted in the deaths of many of his men. He had also vowed not to forget this situation, especially when there was reason to think trouble might be around.

These thoughts prompted Andrej to suspend his gay feeling and to look for cover. Within moments of the decision to hide, he found an older tree just slightly off the path, and placed himself within the hollow shell of its split bark. There he remained for some thirty minutes, or longer, while he attempted to catch his breath, review the important facts, and determine a safe course of action. Just as he was about to continue carefully along this route, he heard voices.

They were speaking Slovenian, which was sweet to his ears, but what they were saying was most distasteful. They were Partisans, bragging about their new position in life. Saying things like, "It's about time we received respect from these fools. Who do they think fought for this country alongside the Allies? And now they all want credit for the victory? Well they had best kiss my red ass. Don't be thanking their Jesus for the victory, thank those of us who were man enough to fight for what was right, and ignore those spineless priests who were only protecting gold for the Church. Tito understands them; we are to eliminate anyone moving back who thinks they are not indebted to the Communist movement!"

Others in the group muttered similar words and encouraged the speaker with smacks on the back. "That's right," he heard muttered, "You either fought with us or you die!"

This exclamation was followed by "That's right, if you didn't starve in the forest, and shiver in caves and dugouts, then you don't deserve the rewards of this victory!"

They were the victors and had a mission yet to fulfill. They carried but two rifles, among the entire group which he counted as about eighteen in all, but had hammers, chains, and strong metal poles. They could commit a lot of destruction with these implements when the situation called for it. And Andrej hated to imagine what it might feel like to be mounted as though a chicken on the spit of that rod. He had better be very careful.

He lingered in his tree until he could determine in which direction this Partisan group was headed. Fortunately, it was the opposite direction to which Andrej was going, so he crept back out onto the path scurrying along for several paces, then stopping and listening. Just as in the long ago days of deer hunting with his brother, he was sometimes startled by noises in the woods which turned out to be squirrels. Then he would continue on down the trail and repeat the entire routine again. Eventually, night was creeping well into the woods and Andrej was both hungry and thirsty, it was time to find a hiding spot for the night. He began by scouting off the trail a considerable distance so that his possible night sounds, or odors from his food supplies, would not warn any group passing by. He further hoped that it was now late enough that these men would have had to crawl into "their own hole."

Soon enough, Andrej did locate an old shack. It was considerably debilitated and looked as though it had been either flooded, or vandalized, or both. Debris was all over the floor, bat and mouse droppings made his steps sticky, and the only hope for sleep would be a hammock. Naturally, that was the only bedding he carried, and soon he had found two existing nails to hold the ends of this makeshift bed. He took care of his personal needs several feet from the cabin, choked down some bread and salami, and finished off the water in his canteen. Naturally, he planned to gather fresh water the next chance he had.

There would be no fire tonight, just cozying up with his backpack and the sides of the hammock. He had food in his stomach and a shelter of sorts. Certainly, he had lived under worse conditions during the last four years. He was going home, and no one was yelling orders at him. He fell asleep thinking how great it was to be a free man.

39

THE TICKING CLOCK

Marica suddenly began clock-watching, calendar-marking, and, in general, became an anxious farmwife. Previously, she was too busy with the baby and the farm to even take note of which day it was, except to go to Church. But, since her husband's phone call she could only concern herself with questions of how many hours, or days, had passed since they spoke, and did this put her close enough to the reunion that he might, just might, walk up their pathway? In the beginning she would laugh these thoughts off as impossible, because not even Andrej could make this trek in a week, or really even in two. Then she endeavored to convince herself that a month would even be too short a span of time for so long a journey. Although, she did often fantasize that someone in a farm truck was approaching Andrej and offering him a ride all the way to Belgrade. Why, with this fantasy, she might expect to receive a call at any moment from the city, with him asking for a ride home. When that call came, she reasoned that she would simply have to hitch their horse to the hay wagon and go! It might not be fancy, but, she was certain neither of them would care.

One afternoon, Marica, decided to go into the library and copy a map which would outline the route Andrej was most likely to be following. That way she could place pins along his supposed trail and incrementally move a pin farther ahead each day. In this manner she hoped to better understand the ups and downs of his journey; it might initially appear a shorter distance than she was thinking, so it was necessary for her to remember where the mountains and rivers were making this trip a challenge. When her pin arrived at such obstacles, she approached the problem in two ways: first, she thought of a probable way of coping with the situation. For instance, could he make a small raft from logs and float down a river; or did he have to walk a great deal farther to find a crossing point or a bridge? And this was a second strategy: she added several days to the estimate for the length of his trip. By so doing, Marica felt she was coping better with the time it was taking for Andrej to get close enough to call home again, or, to walk up that pathway!

But, the weeks turned into more than a month and then began to accumulate enough days for two months to be scratched off the calendar. Marica became increasingly anxious and had trouble answering whenever a neighbor questioned her about the timing of her husband's arrival home. Twice she was called to the phone by her neighbor, only to have her great swell of heart bursting joy fall to the depths of disappointment when the caller turned out to be Vilma, at one point, and Rositha, at another. They were his loving sisters and were themselves motivated by love, as they only wished to hear that he was safe, but they knew nothing of his location. Marica thanked them for their concern and promised that Andrej would telegraph them just as soon as he made it safely home. Then she slipped out of the neighbor's house just as quickly as she could before they would see how consumed with tears she had become. By the second such telephone call, Marica was hardly able to walk back to her farm, as the sobs so wracked her body. And once she was home, it took her a long time to talk away the gloom and horror which were beginning to push out her happy fantasies. She didn't want to be a devastated ragdoll on the floor of the house when her mother brought Valerija home in the afternoon. She wanted to be a strong and happy mommy who would find a way to handle whatever arose and make the little child feel safe and secure with her in charge.

She returned to Belgrade ostensibly for supplies, but in truth, she wanted to know if other husbands had arrived home and if there were tales of what was happening out on the trails leading to home. She knew it could not be good news when others turned away from her as she started to ask how the repatriation was going. Did not thousands of people wish to have their loved ones allowed back into the Kingdom after so vicious a war? Wasn't half of Serbia, Croatia, and Slovenia longing for its sons, daughters, and husbands? "Please," she finally implored the man who sold magazines and newspapers, "Please, tell me what do people nearer the beginning of the pass see and think about the men coming home?"

The newspaper vendor said, "The papers make mention of thousands of people trying to reach Italy and being turned back. They say there is confusion everywhere; no one knows all that is happening. That is all they say, but, if you want my opinion, I believe the Partisans are resentful of the men who did not sacrifice for the Allies; did not fight with them against the Reich."

Marica looked shocked. "What do you mean by that? My husband fought with the Partisans when the Germans invaded right here attacking the Kings' men and the Partisans together, in these streets.

That is how my husband was captured and taken to a German POW camp only being released a few months ago when the war ended. He had no cushy lifestyle, he was starving in the camp and forced to work. He is a hero if you ask me!" And her voice had gotten louder, nearly hysterical, as she fought to protect Andrej from such terrible thoughts.

"Look, madam," he said, "You wanted to know what I have heard and I told you. I probably shouldn't have said a thing, someone may get mad at me, but that is what I think. You be careful who you ask questions of and don't ever mention what I have spoken here. Someone might want to bash my face in for speaking of such things. Just keep your head down. Maybe he'll turn up, I hope he does. The only advice I can give you is check with The Red Cross, they were getting a lot of these POW camp survivors back on their feet and headed home."

This struck Marica as the first good idea she had heard in a long time. "Yes," she said, "I will telegraph their office while I am here in town. Maybe someone there will know what has become of my dear Andrej. Perhaps he is sick, or injured and needing help. Thank you for the brilliant suggestion!" And she used that, perhaps exaggerated word, as it was the first hope she had felt in weeks of longing.

The Royal Palace was in Belgrade. Marica knew that, even though the Allies had worked with Peter II to pull off a coup, the palace was now turned over to the Communists for their role in becoming one of the Allies. Peter II remained the King in Exile, and the will of the country to follow their belief in the Allies, rather than a treaty with Germany, did not matter at the war's ending in terms of this King. He lived for a time in the United States and then in several other countries before residing in England. There were periods of time when funds were raised hoping to reunite Peter II with his Kingdom, but nothing seemed plausible. Tito, a staunch and brutal believer in Communism, was in control of Yugoslavia, as it was now called. He vowed that all men were to be treated the same, and that no one, except himself, was titled any longer. Lands that a family might have owned for six hundred years were taken from this family along with their titles, and any signs that they had ownership over the property.

The "nobility" were likely to end up with no property, and if they had shown even a fleeting sympathy for the Germans, their lives were taken, too. Given the deeds of the Nazis, it is difficult not to feel a kinship with the Communists' reaction to Nazi sympathizers, but in many cases, taking the lives of these royals was a well orchestrated play for their lands.

It is into this atmosphere of righteous hatred of the royals that Andrej came marching home, still believing that he had well served his country and his King, and that he, himself, was an honorable man.

40

THE MARCH HOME CONTINUES

Andrej would have liked to sleep a bit late that next morning in the cabin, but he was surrounded by birds, and it was May. Their chirping with spring fever was vigorous, and before long, Andrej was up and smiling as he too had the need to court his love. He vowed to make more progress today by getting around these Partisans in some fashion which would not require him to hide for hours at a time. He took care of his basic needs, even washing in a little stream, and then crept onto the trail after listening intently to ensure he had no immediate company.

It was a beautiful day, and the birds continued to frolic above him. After about thirty minutes of robust walking, Andrej suddenly noticed that the birds had become silent. He immediately dove into the nearest bushes, and held his breath. If there was a change in the birds' behavior it could mean that a hawk, or some other natural predator, had entered into their environment; or it could also mean that humans, unfamiliar to the birds, were somewhere near. And, as he sat and listened, he heard the sound of sticks snapping, and voices engaged in conversation approaching from the direction in which he was headed. They were not far away. "Those cheepers," he thought, "they saved my life!"

When the group of about six men had passed by, Andrej slowly moved back out onto the path and resumed his trek home. But he had not realized that one of the men had lingered behind as he was answering the call of nature. The two men stared at each other, then Andrej, hoping to keep this man from calling out to his gang, leaped forward and butted him in the head sending them both flying into a pile of rocks and bushes. While the other fellow was dazed, Andrej gagged him by tying the fellow's own shirt around his head and stuffing his mouth with his hat. Then he quickly bound his hands and feet with the ropes this Partisan kept hanging from his belt. He took the man's hammer, also tied to his belt, and charged down the trail to get as far away from this scene as he could before the others would come back looking for their missing friend.

His heart was beating rapidly, but he was pleased to have survived this contact without killing, or being killed. For several miles, as his adrenaline was coursing through his veins, he could not slow down and progressed nicely along the route. Finally, his brain cautioned him to slow down, and to be alert for other possible adversaries along the way. It was good that his brain had warned him, for, only a short distance further on he again had to duck into the underbrush and hide from these militant woodsmen.

"This area is just crawling with Partisans!" he whispered to himself. "I will have to proceed with due caution or I shall be attacked for certain." And he began to crouch-walk for several miles, thinking to make himself less conspicuous than he was at his full height. When he could not handle the back pain any further, he resumed walking upright for about a quarter of a mile. Then he experienced an enormous thud against his left shoulder, and fell flat on his face onto the path and into some brambles.

It seems some Partisans had heard him coming and were waiting while hidden in the brush. As he had passed by their hiding place, they had thrown an enormous rock onto his shoulder. It undoubtedly cracked some bones or vertebrae, knocked the wind out of his lungs, and left him in a helpless heap on the ground. When the four attackers went to examine their catch, for they thought of him as less than human since he wasn't one of them, he was hoisted up off the ground to stare into their faces, and thought that he recognized one fellow from his boyhood. It was a fellow who came every summer to Lake Bled with his family and to whom Andrej and Mojca had given rides in the pletna.

"Aren't you the kid who always liked fishing off the back of the pletna on Lake Bled?" Andrej asked. "My sister and I saw you every summer."

The captor seemed ill at ease, his face getting red and his arms seeming jumpy under this questioning by an enemy. "We did many things as kids, what have you and your sister done to save us from the Nazis?" he asked.

"My sister left this country before the war broke out" he replied, but did not mention where she had gone for fear that the word "Austria" would have incensed these men into believing her to be a Nazi. "But I was a soldier in His Majesty's Army fighting for the Kingdom."

With that remark the other four men began to pummel and beat upon Andrej, immediately bloodying his nose. They shouted, "Death to the King Lover!"

"But," shouted Andrej with all his might, "the King was fighting for all of us when I was in Belgrade; we all loathed the Nazis and battled them with the last ounce of our strength until many of us were captured and imprisoned! I am just walking home after four years in Vienna in a POW camp!"

"Oh, very noble story comrade," said the Partisan. "No doubt you are walking back from Vienna, but you were there fighting for Adolf Hitler and caring nothing for the people who matter. Your family must have had money; don't you own the rights to those boats? Weren't they given to you by the Queen of Austria? You are not for the people, you are a Royalist!"

Then the shouts turned to "Kill the bastard, Tito says we must rid our new country of this type; death to the traitors!"

"No, please!" shouted Andrej, "I am no traitor, I love this country! I have a young wife and a little girl I haven't seen in four years, please, I am not the enemy!"

But at this point the four men found it their pleasure to pound their fists into Andrej until he lost consciousness. He would not be heading home any further this day.

Many miles away, at the farm Andrej dreamed of, a little girl named Valerija came home from visiting with her grandmother, as she did every day. She went into the living room, as her mother was not beside the stove in the kitchen, which was her usual place in the afternoon. And sitting on the floor, next to the fireplace, was her mother. Her mother seemed to be crying so Valerija, a loving child, ran to her and held her asking, "What's wrong, mommy, what's wrong?"

"Oh," replied her mother Marica, "I have been hearing how bad the traveling is for the men coming back from the war, so I started to worry a little too much about your father."

"Do you think he will be alright, Mommy?"

"I hope so darling, your father is a strong and brave man. But we must be prepared for anything because there are still some very bad men out there trying to hurt good people who didn't agree with them about everything during the war. I just don't know what to tell you. But we will wait."

And Valerija said something far wiser than her years and so tender that her mother could not imagine from where the gift of this child came. She said, "If, for some terrible reason, Daddy does not make it back to us, we will always know that he wanted to be here very much. We will plant a tree for him. And because I am half Daddy, when you miss him too much, please just hug me and listen to my heart, for it is the same heart that you are missing."

41

WHERE HAVE YOU TAKEN ME

When Andrej woke up, he felt as though he had been run over by an artillery truck. He could tell that there was crusted blood on his face just by attempting to move facial muscles. And there were similar pulls on his skin from dried blood on his hands, although they were bound behind him. If he could see, there would be even more blood visible, but he was in the bottom of a dump truck, next to other people, and they were all covered with a tarp. Little light was getting in; only enough to reveal vague shapes, but no colors.

As he struggled to turn over, he emitted an involuntary moan. This led to the person next to him whispering, "Are you alive over there?"

It was Slovenian, so Andrej responded, "Yes, I think so." And speaking even so few words hurt his mouth, jaw and throat. All Andrej could think of was the bumpy and painful ride he had taken four years earlier when he was brought to the German POW camp. He hoped the camp to which he was now headed would have guards who were less alert, and he could escape. Maybe from this area he could get as far as his father's farm. He knew if he could get to their farm he could enlist his dad and his brother to help him, or at least to hide him, and when it was safe enough they could get a message to Marica. He felt so low thinking about how much his delay must be troubling her.

Then he whispered back to the body lying against him, "What do you know about where we are being taken?"

And the stranger answered, "Nothing very good. These fools are just seeking corpses for a big death count to please Tito. It doesn't matter who you are; in fact, the more important you might have been, the more they wish to put a bullet in your head. We are just the debris of war; they will use our bodies to fill in caves!" And then he started to laugh and cough and could not stop for some minutes.

Andrej was chilled to the bone by these words, although he had heard such stories at the pass where Slovenians were headed for Trieste. So these stories were actually true, or at least, pervasive enough to be thought so.

Well, he reasoned, I must prepare myself for any eventuality. If there is a way out, I shall take it without hesitation. If not, I must be ready to die with the dignity that would be in keeping with an officer in the King's Royal Army. And he went back to sleep thinking that conserving his energy was the only thing he could accomplish at that moment.

He awoke later as the truck jolted to a stop, and a voice rang out, "Okay, you lazy, bastard traitors, get out of the trucks now!"

Then the tarp was pulled away, and he felt temporarily blinded, as it had been so long since he had seen the light. Blinking and squinting, he managed to take in the scene around him. Perhaps fifty men were in the same truck as he, and all were similarly beaten, bruised, and bloody. It appeared that they were a crop of sorts, and this was the brutal manner in which they were harvested. Now the Partisans were to choose planting them in the ground, out of sight of the Communists. At least as they were pulled out of the truck, their bound hands were retied in front of them so that they could walk.

The camp, it being May, was damp and muddy. Anything at the base of the mountains received an excessive amount of water as the Alpine snows melted and ran downhill in the Spring. To be camping here meant that one would be wet and cold, but at least there was access to water. Unfortunately, this was not a matter that would be of concern to Andrej for long. There were trucks constantly coming into the camp to unload people who had not been part of the Partisans including some Cossacks from the Russian border. These folks were seen as enemies of the Communists, so if they were caught near Yugoslavian soil they, too, were sent to these execution camps. And all along this country there were soldiers trying to get home to Germany. If they were found in the woods, they were added to the numbers in the camps.

But supplies were low. Not only were the camps lacking in food, but also in tents, sleeping bags, latrine equipment and all hygienic products; and critically, they were lacking in bullets. Yet, another demographic must be mentioned which further complicated their supply issues: many of those rounded up and captured were women and children. There was no adequate housing for anyone, let alone privacy for gender separation, or any religious respect.

The Communists had one solution for this problem; prisoners must be eliminated within a day of their capture. Perhaps one bullet would have to serve for more than one death; there had to be creative ways of getting rid of so many people. If they were dead, you did not have to feed them, or house them, or deal with issues around the latrine, or even simple modesty. The only issue which remained was how to kill one hundred people, for example, with six bullets: and so caves had been proposed as solutions to much of this problem.

The next morning, after little sleep and no breakfast, Andrej and the men with whom he had shared the back of the truck, were marched through a neighboring village, to a series of empty mines. The villages were bleak places, dreary and rundown; perhaps they had once been active mining towns, but now were little cared for and dirty. The prevailing color was gray – gray buildings, gray gravel in the streets, and gray curtains in the windows. Small, gray-haired, gray- skinned, people could be seen peeking out of the dirty windows to watch in fear as the prisoners were marched by their homes.

Upon arrival, the prisoners were forced around the edges of these mines at gun point and, additionally forced to be packed in tightly next to each other, around the mine's perimeter. There was not a bit of greenery, or delicate branches, left in view once they were properly packed into the circle. More and more of the prisoners were forced around the edges of the mine shafts, which were much like grooves in the soil, with the top of the caves open to the air. They felt like cattle going to slaughter, for that was what they were, only most of them had enough cognitive ability to know what was about to befall them, where cattle may not.

A few voices were raised in protest, but the majority of the prisoners had been so badly beaten before this time, and left so cold and hungry, that there was little or no fight left in them. They could no longer react in a manner to save themselves, it was learned helplessness. For some, the open gravesites were now almost comforting; they were tired of the struggle, the worry and the suffering.

Andrej was not ready to die. He feared that if he cried out in protest, however, that would earn him the first bullet. And, similarly, if he should struggle, or try to run, he would be singled out for an individual shot. So, he waited anxiously for the deed to occur and prayed to God that somehow he would be spared.

A volley of bullets then rang out spreading along the line of the standing captives as they rimmed the caves. If a bullet did not hit the prisoner directly, it at least hit the prisoner beside him and the force produced enough momentum that all whom the volley peppered with bullets were thrown, wounded or not, into the caves. Andrej found himself on the cave floor. He was alive, yet underneath two other prisoners who were not. He quickly wriggled out from under the bodies, managing to free his hands, just in case of an opportunity. He could hear all around him moaning, praying, and weeping, and he tried to think of what to do next.

Then the most horrible sound arose. He had heard that in previous slaughters the Partisans had blown the caves up to ensure that all were killed as they had so few bullets. Men, women, and children were buried alive. He heard a certain click as a hammer was pressed into the explosive device, then a rumbling, and then it was all over, as rocks, dust and body parts blew into the air and fell back down into the shaft, to be buried for all time. Just as Andrej understood that his time on this earth was up, he pulled the red toque out from inside his shirt where he had kept it since finding it in the streets of Vienna, not far for Julijana's apartment.

He tossed the red hat high into the air, and told himself that if his poor family ever came looking for him they might see the red cap, and know that it had been knitted at his parents' farm on the edge of Lake Bled, and that he was resting in peace.

42

WHERE HAVE ALL THE FLOWERS GONE?

The weeks of waiting for Andrej turned into months. Marica and Valerija went from a state of high anxiety to constant tension. No longer did they anticipate his return at any moment, or that a neighbor would soon call out to them saying that he was on the telephone line. Marica began to fear that a phone call, or any unexpected piece of mail, was going to be the harbinger of tragic news. Someone, perhaps from the new government, or an old army contact, would inform them that Andrej Lovrenc was dead, lost forever.

Yet, she clung to hope as well. If he had been injured, and could not for a time speak, perhaps there could still be a chance that he would be recovered. He would wake up, or get his memory back, and some kind people were sure to send for her. Or that dreaded phone call came, but it was announcing his return to health, he had just remembered who he was, and would now soon be able to travel. These thoughts helped to pull her from the depths of despair. She lived in a cloudy environment where traveling between these two possibilities gave her a quasi state of balance. Like Alice in Wonderland trying to reach the right height for the door she must exit, too much acceptance of his death left her critically despondent or too short to reach the key; and where too much belief that he would still return, left her too anxious to carry on any normal tasks, or as Alice, too tall to fit through the door once the key was at hand.

During her depression Marica knew that there was no pain more exquisite than that of loving someone deeply, with every ounce of her being, with her entire future wrapped around him, and dreams of them as a family, but he cannot be reached. Every dream that had kept Marica going for the last four years, each time she made an improvement in their home, or noted progress in their baby's growth, or thought at all of a future, it was with Andrej and for Andrej. He was her life and joy, and now she was having difficulty breathing; but he was still only missing.

The Red Cross was utterly unable to provide her with hope. They now only repeated that thousands of men had not yet made it home. Perhaps he had been sidetracked along with a great many others; perhaps he had been convinced to make a home for them in Italy where so many refugees wished to go; perhaps she would hear from him sometime soon saying that he was coming to get them; "There would be a new home," one worker had suggested.

But Marica knew what a dependable man Andrej was; if he had not come home by now, or sent word of what was causing his delay, then he wasn't able to. Then her heart switched her mind to blindly seek out the hope again. She continued to obsessively pray for his safe return even while feeling in her heart that he was gone. When others asked her about her husband she could only say "He is missing" and never included the phrase, "and presumed dead."

The air was thinner; the grass was not so green, the breeze felt cruel, not refreshing, or cooling, or sweet. She wore sunglasses now, not to hide her puffy eyes, for swollen they were, but to keep others at a distance; they should not too closely view her pain. It seemed the pain of grief was all she had left of him, and she was not willing to give that up. She decided, with the help of her brother, to give up the farm and move into Belgrade where everything would be close-by, and she did not have to contend with manual labor such as farm repairs and animal husbandry. It would be better for them both. Soon his family, as well as her own, was helping her. But her head and her heart were not right with the universe. Then the years began to pass, and she relaxed a little more knowing that no phone call would ever arrive to tell her that horrible news; there would be no sudden stab of pain, it would remain a gradual loss creeping in without hope of him returning. She always wore black because she would always be a widow.

No man, no matter how kind or helpful could ever convince her to accept a dinner out or a solid laugh. No man could ever make her think it was okay to have fun. She did what was needed for Valerija, and in her heart that was a tribute to him. They had been married and she believed that they were still married. Her husband was only missing.

She frequently spoke to Vilma in London as she thought that the British Allies would eventually possess information regarding Andrej's location. Vilma was filled with sadness about her missing brother, but had no connections with which to help locate him. She was too conflicted about her troubled romance, and soon the fear that she was pregnant, to have the energy for chasing the bureaucrats in search of information on Andrej.

His sister in America, Rositha, was very worried about her lost sibling. With the help of her husband they wrote to a congressman. His office stated that too many people had been reported missing, or displaced, for any of the service representatives, or the Red Cross, to have answers. It was difficult to assess from his message if he thought her cause was hopeless, or that they must simply be patient. But Rositha held thoughts of her missing brother close to her heart. When a short time later she gave birth to her first son, whose middle name was Andrew for her father, she called the boy "little Andrej" after her brother and not her papa. He was a happy little boy and she took many pictures of him which bore her brother's name.

The most important person in the comprehension of what this loss meant to the world was undoubtedly Valerija. Valerija waited with her mother for her father's return. She saw her mother struggle to remain hopeful and turn to God over and over again, only to find deep disappointment. She felt disloyal somehow when she began to truly only remember her father from the photographs her mother had on their tables. She could not remember his voice or recall funny things that they had done together. Soon she could remember nothing but the photos.

When school began she was often asked something about her father by teachers and her classmates. She did what her mother did, and just told them that he had disappeared at the end of the war. Most gave her sympathy and kindness as she didn't have a father, but a few girls said mean things like; "Were your parents even married?" This made her feel angry and a little abandoned, although she knew that her father could not help his absence.

As more time went on, Valerija received support from her uncles, the husbands of her aunts and friends of her mother. She enjoyed this but dreamed of how sweet it would have been to just one time have gone out to a meal in a restaurant with her dad, or to have been pushed on a swing by him, or gone for walks. Years passed, and when she married and gave birth to two beautiful daughters, she felt some pieces of her heart begin to heal; and she always remained close to her mother.

Once enough time had passed without Andrej's return, Marica learned to drive. She corresponded with groups established to find "lost soldiers" and volunteered to help these organizations. There were very few soldiers ever found alive and not many whose bodies were ever recovered either. People did just disappear when the Communist forces did not want them found. More than one hundred thousand went missing in Slovenia, Croatia, and Serbia: mostly in May, 1945. And that is what Marica and even her grandchildren would say about Andrej. He is missing since the end of the war.

43

TWO SISTERS TAKE A TOUR OF EUROPE

After Rositha had her first baby boy she was anxious to complete her family. In part, this was because these boys would be all she had for blood relatives in the United States and because her clock was ticking a bit faster than anyone knew: would her fertility run out if she attempted to space her children by several years as many Americans seemed to do? So in five years Rositha gave birth to three healthy baby boys, and she and Bernard moved into a large Victorian home in Claremont, New Hampshire.

Here they had many tasks, for the once glorious home was a bit run down due to age, with an old-fashioned boiler and several fireplaces. Putting storm windows on the house each fall was a Herculean task, but the price they must pay for the space they wanted in which to raise their three children. The seven bedrooms also represented a valuable asset, as the family was able to put out a sign which read "Rooms" and provide a place for others to sleep. Since the mills in town were running shifts around the clock, it was fairly easy to keep two rooms rented to people who really only wished to have a place to sleep.

Occasionally, they would have a tenant who drank too much or over-stepped his or her boundaries, so they would be asked to leave and soon were replaced. Bernard ran the local Coca-Cola bottling plant and Rositha took part time work in the nearby retail shops. Eventually, she worked a night shift in a factory, traveling out of town by bus to be gone only when her children were sleeping. She was very careful with expenses saving all that she could and certainly avoiding spending money on herself.

Her pleasures came from having plenty of food for the family and frequent correspondence with her surviving kin in Europe, especially Vilma. She'd even had a visit from her beautiful niece Caroline in 1969, as Caroline was following a friend out to California and planning to make that her home. By 1971, twenty-five years after she had left London and last seen her sister, Rositha was headed back for a long overdue visit. Two of her sons were by now married and the third was in the Coast Guard, so it seemed she could spare herself the time.

She flew alone into Heathrow Airport just outside of London. Everything seemed strange as she had never flown before. There was also the time change and the out-of-body sensation of seeing post-war London clean and orderly this many years beyond the Blitz. But the best was yet to come. As she made her way into the airport and was navigating herself through Customs, she heard an unmistakable voice filled with joy cry out "Rositha." Vilma was really there, accompanied by her husband Miha, to take her bags and to drive her to their London townhouse.

The excitement and the tears at that meeting must be appreciated because these two women had grown up sharing a bedroom, sharing a heritage, and then fled Yugoslavia together just as the war broke out. They had been through the Blitz together, shared what food they had in order to survive, and had advised each other through most of the war except for Vilma's adventures with the diplomat and his family on the high seas. They then remained close via frequent air mail correspondence. They had lost the same home, the same parents, and the same brother to say nothing of the destruction of the culture they had loved. But here they both were, alive, well, still attractive and anticipating an adventure.

Rositha revisited key parts of London with Vilma, and then it was time for them to take to the roads. It was too bad to leave the comfortable bedroom in Vilma's town house, but there were places to see. And, like Rositha, Vilma rented out her downstairs rooms for a little income. Miha was so careful with money Vilma joked, "He will probably rent out our bedroom and sleep in the kitchen while we are away!"

But, as the two sisters returned to the airport to fly to Vienna, they decided for once in their lives they would not be frugal. Upon landing, Vilma rented a Mercedes, splitting the bill with her sister, and off they went. They were both attired in modern flared pants, and each had packed several blouses and sweaters with contrasting scarves. This would permit them to be both comfortable and modern.

The streets were too crowded for easy sightseeing so they used a map to find points of interest, including a drive by the area in which Julijana had lived. Seeing that it had been destroyed by the bombings and was still under reconstruction, they continued to follow the route back toward the Slovenian part of Yugoslavia. They believed Andrej must have followed this direction, leading through the Ljubelj Pass, as he was walking home.

Naturally, this passageway was by now a modern road with traffic signals and directions for rest stops along the way. They spoke of Andrej more than they had expected to, but it felt good to let out the thoughts and feelings. It was still impossible to believe that he had just "disappeared," and horrible to conceive of what brutality he must have faced.

Rositha said, "I need to go over this ground with my own eyes just to have a sense of where he traveled. I remember when we were little rolling down the hill with him and then swimming in the lake so we wouldn't have to carry so much water to the house for bathing. He was a dear brother."

Vilma said, "I have been thinking the same thing. I always wished we could have looked for him ourselves but it was impossible at that time. There were too many displaced people wandering and lost."

They sighed almost simultaneously and then continued to comment on the scenery. The mountainous areas were still not too built up and the trees grew perfectly straight and were lush. It was a pretty ride but almost boring in its symmetry. As soon as they crossed over into Yugoslavia they would have to show their papers and get some coffee. They continued to talk, speaking of how they were almost like twins having each given birth to a first child just one week apart in the same year. And they regretted that Roger and Caroline could not have grown up together and been the close friends that they were. But surviving the war had dictated many of their decisions; choices had been limited.

Soon they were taking a room for a night in someone's home and then driving on to Bled. They wanted to see their brother Ivan and place flowers on their parents' graves. They posed for pictures in front of the pletna and ate lunch in the center of the town. They made a date with a cousin who was about their age and whom they had always loved. She was a beautician but confessed she could not make them young again. They all laughed and cried to hear this.

After a few days, it seemed time to continue the trip. After consulting the map, Vilma and Rositha decided to use the less-traveled older roads and head for Trieste. Many of those fleeing Yugoslavia had headed here to the part of Italy closest to their home, as this would have placed them under the auspices of the Americans rather than the Communists. Their European trip would be completed by a short time on the Italian coast.

Their windows were wide open as they sped along with their scarves flowing in the breeze. In a couple of hours, they again felt the need for coffee and stopped, looking for a café in an old mining town. They decided to hunt for coffee on foot in order to stretch their legs. Looking around they felt a bit dejected as the circumstances surrounding them appeared fairly dire. The houses were not well maintained, many had a permanent gray cast to their paint, and the few people that they saw out were ashen skinned.

"Well, no doubt a hardworking community, no frills," Rositha said.

"Yes," replied Vilma. "We have many areas in the United Kingdom that are over-shadowed by the gloom of the coal mines."

Then they spotted a wooden structure which appeared to be half coffee shop, half house. There were a few small tables and chairs on its front porch and commercial signs advertising soda and ice cream on a stick. It didn't look clean, but it didn't look too bad either. They headed toward it as there really were no other choices.

No one greeted them so they peeked inside the open door. It looked like a household kitchen but there was a long wooden bar along the left with four stools. They called out hello in Slovenian.

That is when someone stirred in the corner and made a gurgling sound followed by footsteps from another direction.

A woman, approximately their age, came down the corridor presumably from inside the house. She asked, "What may I do for you?"

Vilma said, "We would like two coffees with cream if that is possible?"

"Certainly" replied the woman as she went to a machine and began adding things. Then she turned to the person in the corner and asked, "And Joseph, would you like a little coffee-milk?"

He replied with a nod and a guttural sound. She seemed to accept this as an affirmative response and began to prepare a heavy plastic mug for him.

Vilma would never be rude but, without even thinking, she drew in her breath and said, "Poor man."

"Yes," the woman said. "We have been caring for him since the war ended. We call him Joseph as he seems a saint to us. We don't really know who he is or what exactly happened to him. He was so badly hurt when he crawled into town that he wasn't expected to live. But he did, he just can't communicate much of anything, but he is easy to be around."

Rositha asked, "May I go close to him?"

"Oh sure," said the proprietor. "I'm sure he would enjoy the attention. Go right ahead."

Rositha crouched on the floor next to the man. She smiled and said a few Slovenian words to him. He smiled back and she patted his shoulder. She was certain that as damaged as he was, with scars everywhere, facial bones that looked collapsed, and just a fringe of white hair, it was not her brother. These eyes were blue not hazel, but for one moment she wasn't quite certain, and her heart almost broke.

Before they left, she gave the woman as much cash as she had and simply said, "It is as though you were taking care of my brother. Bless you."

And they departed.

Joseph shakily groped inside his shirt until he pulled out some scraps of red yarn which he used to wipe tears from his cataract-covered eyes.

44

SEPARATING FICTION FROM NONFICTION

Many readers believe it is important to know which parts of this book actually happened and which bloomed from the writer's imagination. I will now set the record as straight as I am able.

Rositha Por Adams (1912 – 1998) of Claremont, New Hampshire was the author's mother-in-law beginning in 1970. Just as described here-in she was the mother of three boys: Roger, Steve, and Bradley. She had also met her G.I. husband, Bernard C. Adams, during the war in London where they were married. Up until her marriage she had been living with her youngest sister Marjana (called Vilma in the story) in London, to which they had fled around 1937, hoping to escape much of the war. Most of the details of Rositha's life are based on her accounts to the family. Her working for the Wedgwoods is true, and she did almost stand Bernard up on their blind date, but he waited so long for her that she relented and joined him. She did not return to Europe for twenty-five years following the war, and when she did it was to tour with her siblings Marjana, Angela, and Janez plus Miha (1971). Her sister Fanika had passed away and their brother Lovro (Andrej in the story) was missing since the end of the war. Rositha had completed all the schooling available to her and could have been a teacher if not for the war. During her adult life there was evidence that she had recovered on her own from Tuberculosis and had suffered with serious anemia from which she also recovered. She and Marjana, who also had anemia, survived two years of bombings in London called the Blitz. They had all grown-up in beautiful Bled, Slovenia within view of Lake Bled. The incident at the coffee shop in the mining town with Vilma was fictitious; there has been no trace of Lovro to date.

Marjana Por Hajnzic [Vilma] (1914 – 2011) story was reported to the author by her only daughter, Caroline, although the author met Marjana in 1983 when she, her husband Roger Adams, and their infant son, Andrew Adams, stayed with her in London accompanied by Rositha. The author also learned about Marjana from discussions with Rositha. At that time Lovro's [Andrej's] widow, Marica, their daughter Valerija, and her two daughters, now Marija Andjelkovic Novakovic, and Aleksandra Por Marcetic, were also visiting. (These last two names are the granddaughters of Lovro.) Marjana did flee Belgrade on the SS Strathaird with a family for whom she worked, and they were fired upon by torpedoes. She had also made trips back to Bled without Rositha early on as she had a serious boyfriend there whom she had planned to marry. But on one of her visits home, her sister Angela informed her that he had a child now by another woman and Marjana broke off their engagement. It seems that the man then took his own life. It is speculated that while recovering from this trauma, Marjana was more willing to take the risks of traveling with the diplomat's family. Details of Marjana's further romance are a combination of reports from Caroline and the author's imagination. Caroline resulted from this relationship with "Samuel." The tale of Marjana meeting Miha is correct and he was a loving stepfather to Caroline. Caroline had no contact with her bio-dad after age two when he married a woman other than her mother. His behavior was much like the character of Samuel. Caroline did not go to see him until she was sixty-five years old thinking to spare her mother pain, but, he was by then, not cognitively aware. One day while Caroline was little, her mother dressed her in her best clothing, with a new red bow in her hair, had her practice curtseying, then brought her to meet the widow of Alexander I, Peter II's mother, "Queen Maria" who was living in London. Caroline was also raised in the local Slovenian community her mother found in London and which was associated with their church. Caroline lived in the USA much of her adult life, although now dwells in London in the family townhouse.

Janez Por [Ivan] (1904 – 1980) was actually the oldest of the Por children. It is true that he was working for the railway and was in a serious accident in his early twenties. His skull was fractured requiring the insertion of a steel plate. This kept him from fighting in the war and was a lifelong impairment. He did marry however, had a son Ivo (1942 – 2017), and I believe a daughter who died in an accident. We were fortunate to meet Ivo's son, Marko Por, who is a tennis coach for Tenis Slovenija, born in 1971. He and his family seem to be thriving in Slovenia.

Lovro Por [Andrej Junior] (1906 – 1945?) was important to write about. He was raised as a good Catholic, as they all were, and he was loyal to his king and country. He moved to Belgrade to serve in the King's Royal Army, and this is where he met and married his wife, Marica and had baby Valerija. As mentioned in the paragraph above regarding Marjana, Valerija had two daughters and her eldest one, Marija, was most helpful in researching this book. There were many transatlantic calls, emails and photographs needed to tell the whole story. No one living knows what Lovro went through in the Nazi POW camp. The exact circumstances of his death remain a mystery. The author used stories written by others, and accounts of a few survivors, to describe a likely scenario of the poor man's last days. He is one more star in the universe of senseless losses created by war.

Fanika Por Buncic [Mojca] (1908 – 1947). Moved to Belgrade from Bled and was married to a man named Stevo. During the war, both her home and that of Marica (Lovro's wife) were bombed, although it was cancer which cut short her life. Physically she looked so much like Rositha that it makes photographs a bit difficult to identify. She was not connected to the pletna nor was she a war hero, but a well-loved older sister to Rositha, Marjana and Angela. She did not immigrate to Australia although it is true that many Yugoslavians did so because moving to the USA had become difficult. The story of the rescue of the people held in the concentration camp outside of Lintz was fictitious, but that horrible camp, Mauthausen, was real.

Angela Por [Julijana] (1910 - 1984) Angela had a son, but no one in the family seemed to know the father's identity. Angela spent a great deal of time in Austria from an early age. This baby had been born in 1932 when she was but twenty-two. Her sisters all speculated that he was German, based on his looks, his name (Hansi), and their love of intrigue. After the war Angela married a man named Franz and they lived in a suburb of Vienna where she had a beauty shop. Again, it is speculated that Franz might have had connections to the Nazis. This time the thoughts arise from his name, his location, and his profession as an artist who was very good at reproducing almost anything. Unfortunately, Hansi, an architect, is no longer living nor does he have children to interview.

Following these descriptions of the six children it should be stated that **Andrej Por [Andrej Senior]** (1868 – 1950) was the father of these children. His life was much as described in the book although not connected to the pletna. He was a roofer and a farmer. He donated most of his farm land to the Catholic Church for use as a cemetery and that is where he and his wife, his son Janez, and grandson, Ivo are interred. There is a story that Napoleon was involved with his family and that Andrej was captured by the Partisans but managed to escape and return home. **Ivana Pogacar Por [Justa]** (1881 -1939) was well represented in the book. She did die just as WWII was about to begin. Her youngest sister (from a large family) was a friend to her nieces. She is said to have been very wealthy and traveled often to see them all. She was Aunt Helena.

THE PLETNA

The stories of the pletna and their importance to Lake Bled are true. They have deeded ownership dating back to Queen Maria Theresa. But the Por family is not the owner of the deed. However, the author and her husband, Rositha's oldest son, Roger Adams, were fortunate enough to meet the owners of the pletna and to rent an apartment from them while doing research for this book. They were enthusiastic about assisting in tracking down relatives, the location of the family gravesite, and teaching us much of the folklore of the area including the tale of the "Bell at the Bottom of the Lake."

Their kindness and assistance has continued and influenced this story; the names "Mojca," "Vid," "Manca," and "Zala" used within the story are a tribute to them. They became among our dearest new "family."

Antoija Music (ne: Mandelc) Matriarch

Mojca Music and Robert Krasovec

Vid, Manca and Zala Krasovec

Please see photos on my website:

https://www.getbooksbycindy.com

Names in [ ] next to actual names, represents how their name appeared in the book.

ADDENDUM
PETER, THE LAST YUGOSLAVIAN KING

There was a Prince Regent serving as the King of Serbs, Croats and Slovenes as war was finally bursting through the skies in Eastern Europe. Children watched with admiration and fear as the German Luftwaffe circled in practice flights over their playing fields creating a loud droning sound so deep it made their hearts vibrate. Little by little there appeared to be foreign military living in the midst of their people and urging the young to join them in their war game practices. These soldiers always seemed to have new uniforms, plenty to eat at their barracks, and were willing to share. There was also a shift in ethnic values: one day it was not so popular to be known as a German, and the next day, being German held status even though few had forgotten the troubles of The Great War which had ended roughly twenty years before.

Prince Regent Paul, either misjudging the wishes of his people or, because he was convinced that his country, and he, would be better served by the Germans, signed a declaration on March 25, 1941 committing Yugoslavia to be a friend of Germany and a member of the Tripartite Pact. This signature did not maintain the status quo but acted as a catalyst bringing the people of Belgrade, and all Allied supporters in the Kingdom, to the streets in protest.

It was at this point that, anticipating such a reaction was possible, the British had been cultivating a relationship with the Kingdom thinking to limit the spread of the war. They acted strategically and quickly to stage a coup d'état in which the seventeen-year-old King Peter was proclaimed of age, thus displacing Regent Paul. In one report, Peter had to slide down a drainpipe to be freed from the castle, but once he was seen, the people, including the Regent's guards, declared their loyalty to him.

General Simovic led troops, supported by the British, up to young Peter and announced "Your Majesty, I salute you as King of Yugoslavia. From this moment you will exercise your full sovereign power." The crowd and Belgrade rejoiced. Many who showed up to salute the King were obviously in favor of the Allies, as they were waving French and British flags. The King was happy to accept his duty and drove his own car up and down the streets of Belgrade to the cheers of his subjects. That same day he would swear in a new government which was headed by General Simovic and had representatives from at least eight of the divergent political factions of those days including Catholics and Muslims. The only organizations which did not have a seat at the table were the Yugoslav Radical Alliance, Yugoslav Communist Party, and Ustashe.

And as they had fled Belgrade, the camaraderie and joy expressed the day Peter II received the crown, was quickly reported to Hitler who believed he was to have been favored by a contract with Yugoslavia. This made him angry, so angry that in fact, he altered his plan of attack called Operation Barbarossa, and his army simultaneously attacked both Yugoslavia and Greece. This time the children would not be enjoying themselves as they chased the shadows of the incoming planes. This time they would run from the planes in terror as the Luftwaffe repeatedly bombed Belgrade killing thousands of people. Their playing fields would be filled with craters and debris. The vibrations of the planes would be joined by sounds of a piercing whistle and then an explosion. Fear would dictate when they might open their eyes, or peek out to see what the bombs had split; what was left of their worlds and their friends.

Then the attack was joined by Bulgaria, Hungary and Italy all invading Yugoslavia. These attacks meant that areas already under the Nazis' powers, or the Tripartite, would invade with equipment intended for destruction and conquest. These proved to be overwhelming forces for smaller armies and farmers wishing to resist with pitchforks and hammers.

Little wonder that Yugoslavia was forced to surrender. King Peter II had held his throne from March 27, to April 6, 1941. He was rescued, along with General Simovic and some of his ministers, by the Allies and taken first to rural Greece. Two of the ministers had been killed during the fighting with the Germans, and several chose to stay behind. The British then flew him to British ruled Jerusalem where he hoped to serve as "King in Exile" until the war was over, or Yugoslavia was returned by the Allied Forces. But, as he was being brought to safety, the men who had sworn to guard and protect him and the Kingdom were engaged in bloody combat. This is when Andrej was captured to spend four years as a German POW. Yugoslavia was then annexed in pieces to the invaders and to puppet governments of the Germans.

The King in Exile did not suffer like his countrymen. He was wined and dined as many people considered it an honor to have royalty in their homes. While those in exile tried to set up a framework for their eventual return it was not to happen. But such was not immediately known.

When Peter was brought to London, he was still seventeen years old and treated like a war hero. He became the symbol of his country's fight for freedom and their alliance with the Allies. But, after a short time of trying to raise troops to go back into Yugoslavia and fight for the Allies, it was determined that there were very few soldiers available. Yugoslavia seemed to have the least resources of any of the deposed leaders.

Then a guerrilla force emerged called the Chetniks, lead by Colonel Draza Mihailovic. They were fighting the Germans and King Peter's men found a way to communicate with them, tying them to the Allies. But things became more complicated when Peter heard that a group called the Ustashe was committing atrocities on Serbs, expelling many from the country and forcing others to convert to Catholicism. The small cabinet Peter had held onto in exile, which so proudly represented multiple factions, was not able to be in the same room together. The Serbs could not believe the Croats and the Croats could not tolerate the Serbs.

Because of vicious reprisals promised by the Germans for every Axis soldier killed, the Chetniks were less willing to attack them, while the Partisans, who were better organized, seemed willing to take risks. Eventually, the Partisans proved far more able to tie down the German and Italian troops, and were seen as true to the Allies. This was difficult for the King, who had put much faith in the guerrilla tactics by "his" Chetniks, and knew that they had disappointed the British.

Peter completed his education at Cambridge University, and while still attempting to be of service in exile, worked with both the Greek King and Czechoslovak-Polish leaders. There was always discussion by this group of working into a "Balkan Union." Then Peter hoped to strengthen his country's future by connections to the Soviet Union and the United States. He met many important people during his diplomatic journeys such as President Franklin D. Roosevelt, and a countryman named Tesla. They treated him respectfully but he was never able to overcome political problems he had blamed primarily to the Chetniks.

Chetnik massacres against Croats and Bosnian Muslims turned many Yugoslavians against the King. The intense Serb nationalism of the Chetniks also disturbed Allied politicians. A decision was made that Croatian Communist Josip Broz Tito would provide a more stable government to Yugoslavia, and his Partisans had been most helpful in ending the war. No one knew of the massacres and atrocities which these Communists would wreak upon their non-Communist brothers at the war's end. King Peter II was left without his kingdom.

Made in United States
Orlando, FL
21 April 2022

17060632R00168